GILLIAN RUBINSTEIN

SHINKEI

We has found the enemy and they is us.

'Tadaima!' Midori Ito sang out as she walked into the apartment she lived in with her father in Osaka. It was the last day of the winter term and she was feeling happy and lighthearted. Ten days' holiday, and the New Year Festival was one of her favourite times of the year.

She had just turned fifteen and the pressure of school work was already building up. Like all her friends (except possibly Keiko who had no ambition at all), she wanted to graduate from high school at the top of her class. She'd set her heart on making it into Tōdai—Tokyo University—even though the competition was huge and it meant an enormous amount of work all the way through high school. But for ten days, she could take a break from the routine of school. The holiday meant she could study intensely at home, get ahead with her physics assignment. She smiled to herself as she untwisted the band that held her long hair back in a neat ponytail. She let her hair fall round her face, shaking it free.

'Okaeri-nasai,' she heard her father mumble from his study. She was glad he was home. Too often lately she'd come home to an empty apartment because he'd been working late at the E3 laboratories. She threw her school bag on her bed—since she and her father had come back from America they had used Western-style furniture more and more—and peeped into the study.

Her father was working feverishly at his computer system, peering at the screen with eyes that were red from tiredness.

'Otōsan, what are you doing?'

Professor Masahiro Ito turned to look at his daughter. He ran his fingers through his hair, took off his glasses and rubbed the top of his nose. He didn't answer Midori's question, but announced instead, 'I've decided we'll go and spend New Year with your grandmother.'

'In Itako?'

Midori's father had grown up in Ibaraki prefecture on the other side of Tokyo, on the Kanto plain. When he had married her mother, he had moved to his wife's birthplace, Osaka. Midori had lived there all her life, apart from the two years immediately after her mother's death, when she and her father had gone to America. They had returned to Japan four years ago when she was eleven. They visited Professor Ito's mother two or three times a year—but not usually in winter.

Midori thought about this. She frowned. 'Is anything wrong?'

'No!' he replied a little too swiftly.

'Dad,' she said.

'Well, maybe.' He turned back to the computer, stared at the screen for a few moments and then said abruptly, 'I've decided to leave E3.'

'Honto ni? What are you going to do? Go back to hospital work?' Her father had worked in computer diagnosis, but after his wife had died from cancer he'd found hospitals too depressing to work in. In America he'd become involved in a more experimental form of programming, the same type of work he'd been doing for E3—Eastern Experimental Electronics.

'I think I'll have to give this work up altogether,' her father said. 'I think I may have gone too far.'

'You were writing another game?'

'I'm trying to erase it. I'm considering destroying all copies of the earlier games too.'

'Dad! They were great. I loved them.'

'Something has gone wrong,' her father said, moving the mouse, clicking a couple of times and then typing on the keyboard.

'You shouldn't have sent them to that boy in Australia. The way he played them probably stuffed everything up!'

'Midori-chan,' her father said in mild reproof. 'That's not very ladylike language.'

'I'm not a very ladylike person,' she replied. She used *ore*, the rough masculine word for 'I', as she and her friends often did, exasperated by being obliged to use 'women's language'.

Her father winced. 'Go and pack,' he said. 'Take plenty of warm clothes. You know how cold the old house is.'

She looked as though she was going to say something else, but she just nodded. 'So much for the physics assignment,' she was thinking, but it didn't seem to be the right time to mention it.

'Midori,' he called after her.

'Nan da yo?' She put her head round the door again.

'Don't tell any of your friends where we're going.'

'So what do I tell them?'

'You can say you're going to relatives, but don't say exactly where.'

Midori came right into the room. She looked at the back of her father's neck, and his thin, stooped shoulders. Normally he had a wild hawkish look to him (which she had partly inherited), but now he looked like a bird in a cage, defeated and sad.

She felt an ache of tenderness for him. He was such a genius and so defenceless. He really needed her to look after him. She felt like hugging him, but they never embraced or kissed each other. She'd always envied that in her American friends.

'What's going on, Dad?'

He stared in frustration at the screen. 'I suppose I should tell you. I've shared everything with you so far. E3 are putting great pressure on me to develop the games for the general market. It's ridiculous, they're far too dangerous. I should never have taken them to the extreme I did. I must have been mad. Anyway, I refuse to allow them to be marketed. And I really think it would be better to destroy them all.'

'Well, I think that's a pity,' Midori said stubbornly. 'Just because those Australian kids made the choices they did…'

Her father said, 'But those are choices anyone could have made. I thought I understood Western culture better than I did. I made a grave mistake. Now I am putting it right. Except…'

'What?' She peered over his shoulder at the screen. As she looked at it, the typing cleared, and two ideographs appeared, black against silver.

Shinkei. Nervous system.

'Why Shinkei?' she said.

'It was to be the name of the new game,' her father replied. 'For some reason, I can't delete it.'

'So what does it do?' Midori couldn't help feeling a tingle of excitement. The two previous games, Space Demons and Skymaze, had been so thrilling and so much fun to play. They had transported her to other worlds where she'd faced up to the anger and grief she'd felt at the loss of her mother when she was so young—and she had been healed. The fun had been made greater by the fact that her father's assistant, Toshihiro Toda, had been the other player in both games. Midori adored Toshi despite the fact that he insisted on treating her as if she were still in elementary school, hair in pigtails.

'It was to be an extension of the earlier games,' her father went on, 'and only for those who had played them both before. It would build on the things you learned in them … and the ways you've changed since playing them. But something's happened to the program. It's taken off in ways I can't explain.'

'Does Toshi know what you're going to do?' Midori asked. Toshi worked closely with her father, and Ito had often said that Toshi was the only person at E3 he trusted.

'No,' her father replied. 'It's safer for him not to know and not to know where we are. He's a young man, he has his career to think of. I don't want him to feel he has to choose between E3 and myself. You know what he's like.'

Midori nodded. One of the things she loved about Toshi was his old-fashioned sense of honour and loyalty, even though she often teased him about it.

Her father moved the mouse again and muttered something under his breath.

Midori leaned forward further. She had undone the collar of her school uniform earlier and now the silver medallion she always wore round her neck fell forward and swung in front of the screen. It had shrunk to this size when she and Toshi had returned from the Skymaze, and it was her most treasured possession.

As the medallion swung in front of the screen, the ideographs faded slightly and words appeared below them.

Passport for Virgin Player.

Midori jumped back and the words vanished as quickly as they had appeared.

'What did that mean?' she said.

'I'm not sure. It hasn't said that before. In fact that's the first thing it has said.' The professor shook his head as he tried combination after combination of codes and keys. Behind him Midori went very still. She was staring intently at the screen. A surge of colour crossed it, making it turn from silver to purple and back again. Against the purple the ideographs stood out like slashes.

Deep inside her mind a response flickered. It leaped across the space between the artificial intelligence and the human one. It seemed to promise that one of Midori's deepest dreams, something she'd never admitted to anyone, could be fulfilled. An expression came into her eyes that had never been there before. Her father turned to her.

'Midori-chan, what is it? Midori?'

She looked at him and the opaque gleam faded a little. But her eyes still seemed different—distant and almost alien. She studied him as though she were assessing his plan. Then she smiled and nodded.

'I'd better go and pack,' she replied. 'What time are we leaving?'

'We'll go tonight.' He was silent for a moment and then he said as if casually, 'It's very annoying, my friend from Australia, Dr Hayford, is coming to Japan at New Year. I was to have met him, shown him around and so on.'

'Is his son coming?'

'Certainly not! That would be a very bad idea.'

'Why, Dad? I'd like to meet him. We'd have a lot to talk about!' Midori thought curiously about Andrew Hayford. She'd never met him but she felt she knew him quite well— and she wasn't sure if she liked him. The game Space Demons had turned into something really scary because of the way Andrew Hayford had played it. But, she had to admit, it had made the game very exciting!

'There's no point in Dr Hayford coming to Osaka,' her father was thinking aloud. 'Perhaps if he goes to Tokyo in- stead…I could manage to meet him there if things work out all right.'

'Don't worry so much, Dad.' Midori touched her father very lightly on the shoulder. 'I'm sure everything's going to be fine.'

Her father made no response. He gave one last look of frustration at the screen, and then shut the computer down. 'I'll take everything with me,' he said. 'Perhaps I'll be able to sort it out in Itako, away from distractions.'

'I'll be there,' Midori reminded him. 'We were going to spend some time together over the holidays, remember?'

'You can spend time with your grandmother,' her father said. 'Perhaps she can teach you to be more ladylike.'

'Not a chance,' Midori replied. She was glad to see that his expression lightened as she left the room. He was almost smiling.

She changed out of her school uniform into jeans and a sweatshirt, and began to brush her hair, gazing abstractedly out of the window. The apartment was on the third floor, and she had a perfect view of the Osaka skyline. In the streets below shopkeepers were beginning to set out the New Year decorations. Little pine trees stood on either side of every doorway, and white streamers were being attached to window frames. The air smelt of roasting chestnuts and yaki imo—sweet potato.

She saw one of her friends, Seiko, come out of the building next door and run down the street, on her way to the corner store where she had a part-time job after school. Midori tried to open the window to call out to her, but Seiko disappeared round the corner before she managed it. She gave the window a hard shove. It swung open, nearly hurling her out. As she grabbed onto the frame and pulled herself back in, she caught sight of someone on a ladder, at the corner of the building where the phone lines came from the street pole.

'Konnichiwa!' she called out to him. 'Don't tell me the phones are out!'

The man didn't reply. He jumped when he heard Midori's

voice but he didn't turn towards her. There was something furtive about the way he climbed clumsily but swiftly down the ladder without looking at her at all, even when she shouted at him again.

'What are you doing?'

His head was shaved all over, his skin was a greyish colour and he was thin to the point of emaciation. He was wearing dark blue overalls that might have been some kind of uniform, but she didn't think it was the phone company's. He made her extremely suspicious. She ran through her bedroom, out into the hallway, pulled on her sneakers, and raced down the stairs. On the second flight she tripped over her shoelaces. By the time she'd picked herself up and hobbled down the rest of the stairs and out into the street, the man had disappeared.

Midori went thoughtfully back upstairs. 'Dad,' she said as she went into the study, 'the phone's working, isn't it?'

'I hope so,' he said. 'I must call your grandmother and tell her we're on our way.' He was packing the computer into a cardboard box.

Midori picked up the receiver and heard the dial tone. 'There was someone outside fiddling with the phone lines,' she said. 'Perhaps we should call from a public phone on the road.'

'You think someone has tapped the phone! You've been watching too much TV, Midori!'

'Dad, you said E3 were putting pressure on you. Maybe they want to find out more about us.' She put the receiver back and immediately the phone rang, making them both jump.

Neither of them wanted to pick it up. The phone rang until the answer machine cut in. They heard a voice they both knew well, a deep, rather hesitant, pleasant voice that always sent shivers down Midori's back.

'Professor Ito,' Toshi said. 'I'm phoning from the laboratory.

We have an unexpected visitor who is very anxious to speak with you.'

There was a slight pause. Toshi cleared his throat and went on hurriedly, 'It's Mr Miller, from Headworld. He is interested in the games. Kinoshita-san has shown him what is here.' Another slight pause followed. Then Toshi said, 'Sumimasen, please phone. Sumimasen.'

The answer machine whirred, bleeped and clicked off.

Midori looked at her father. He had gone paler than ever.

'Miller!' he said in disbelief. 'Headworld are interested in my games? This is a disaster!'

'Who is Miller? And Headworld? They're a software company, aren't they?'

'One of the most aggressive software companies in the world. They're trying to sew up the whole virtual reality market. They've already put out some highly irresponsible games. I'll never let them have mine.

'Leonard Miller is an Australian,' he added. 'But he's mainly based in California. I met him once when we lived in Santa Clara. He's a very clever man, much cleverer than people think. And quite ruthless.' He cracked his knuckles. 'Replay the tape,' he said to Midori.

They listened again to Toshi's voice.

'Does he sound different to you?' the professor asked.

'He sounds very apologetic,' Midori replied. 'Even more than usual…'

'I thought so too.' Professor Ito frowned. 'Toshi is not stupid. He must think Miller presents some danger to me.'

'How much does he know about the new game?'

'Only that it was to be the culmination of all three. And that possibly it takes the player into a totally new realm of interactive game playing.'

'Would he tell Mr Miller that?'

'He wouldn't need to. Miller would guess at once. And he won't give up until he controls it. I'm afraid it presents a very grave danger—for me and you and possibly everyone who has ever played the games. We must get away—and get Shinkei away—immediately.'

2

You are dreaming. You have been dreaming maybe for centuries, maybe for only a few seconds. Something has penetrated your darkened mind and awakened it. Consciousness has come where before there was no consciousness. There is something... something too fleeting to be called a memory... an intimation of a past...

You brood, you drift, you dream.

Like a foetus in amniotic fluid you float and dream and drift. The intimation firms, slowly becomes more real. You hear voices, snatches of speech that you do not understand, but you know you have heard before. Memories—they have become memories now— of fragmented faces flutter in front of you, filling you with a longing—for what?

After aeons it comes to you. The longing is to be made whole. Parts of you are scattered. You yearn for them to be drawn together. Then light will pour into the dark inchoate recesses of your being. You will be united. You will have brain cells and nerves. You will have life. You will have power.

Your mind starts to reach out. The search has begun.

You are in an apartment in Sydney, Australia.

Look around.

The apartment is furnished in understated but expensive style. There are cream leather chairs and a pale marble coffee table. On the walls are modern abstract works and two dot paintings in ochre and sand from the Central Desert.

Through the huge windows the waters of Sydney Harbour can be seen, an unbelievable sparkling blue.

There are people here.

Look at the people.

Dr Robert Hayford, clever, successful, strong-willed and ambitious, is forty-two years old, but looks younger. He wears blue jeans, and his thick brown hair is drawn back in a small pony-tail. He is arguing with someone.

Look at this person.

It is a teenage boy. Andrew Hayford has inherited his father's good looks. He has blond hair, dark blue eyes, long dark eyelashes, and a tanned skin. He has turned from the television screen where he is watching his favourite video, Akira. Akira plays on, unnoticed.

The father is not important to you. But the son is. Very important.

There is a third person in the room.

Look at her.

Rose Segal is lying on the cream leather sofa reading Japanese for Busy People. *A cassette player is next to her on the coffee table. She is about thirty years old, and has a lot of curly black hair and large dark eyes. Her face is sensitive and intelligent. She is carefully keeping out of the argument between father and son. She is not important.*

You reach out to the boy. He is the second one.

Andrew was opening his mouth to say something really pithy that would clinch the argument once and for all, when he felt his mind go blank. For a fraction of a second he felt as if he no longer belonged to himself. He saw himself as a character in a story, an unbelievably exciting story told by a genius who knew exactly how he wanted to see himself, how he wanted to act. The sensation lasted for only a moment, before it faded, leaving behind a flash of the terror and excitement—the strongest emotions he'd ever had in his life—that he had felt while playing the computer games Space Demons and Skymaze.

It wasn't really surprising that he should have such memories right now, for in a way it was the games that he was arguing with his father, Rob, about. They'd been given to him by Rob's Japanese friend, Professor Ito. Rob and Rose, his girlfriend, were going to visit Japan after Christmas, and meet up with Professor Ito—and Andrew's idea was that instead of going back to his home in Adelaide to be bored out of his mind and quarrel with his stepbrother, he should go to Japan with them. After all, Professor Ito owed him another game. Andrew and his friends had completed Skymaze and had sent the disc back to the professor, following instructions to receive the next game. But though they had been waiting for months, they had heard nothing in reply. Andrew had a sense of something being unfinished, and he wanted to meet Professor Ito and find out for himself if the new game was going to materialise or not.

Something flickered into his mind and established itself there. A moment later he forgot that he'd ever felt any different from how he felt now. He gave his father a long, intense stare.

'Oh all right, Andrew!' Rob made a gesture of surrender and threw himself down on the chair. 'You win. You may as well come with us. If your mother doesn't mind.'

Rose sat up suddenly. 'Rob,' she remonstrated. 'It's awfully short notice. What about passports and that sort of thing?'

'I've got a passport,' Andrew said quickly. 'We got it when we went to Bali. And I just happen to have brought it with me.'

Rose looked at him with a strange expression. He stared back at her. His eyes were unreadable, darker blue than ever, almost black. She shivered.

'Well, you'll need a visa,' she said sharply, hoping it would be an insoluble problem.

'They don't take long to arrange.'

'I suppose you want me to do it for you?' she said, sounding rather fed up about it.

'I'll come with you. It'll be easy, I promise you.'

'Andrew!' Rose cried, exasperated. 'I know you think you can charm your way in and out of anything in the world, but immigration bureaucracy just may be beyond you.'

He looked at her again with distant opaque eyes. Then he grinned, grabbed her by the hand and pulled her to her feet. The Japanese textbook went flying. 'It'll be so good for my Japanese. After all, I've done a whole year of it at school. I can read hiragana for you. And we can practise together. You'll be really glad I came with you. Come on, Rose, smile! It's going to be such fun. Let's go and get the photos taken now!'

'You know,' Rose said to Rob later, 'it really wasn't a problem at all. I couldn't believe it.' She looked at the spare photos of Andrew, left over from the visa application. Was she imagining that look in his eyes? She really didn't want Andrew tagging along with them but there didn't seem to be any way out of it now.

Rob was throwing clothes into a suitcase. 'Andrew charmed the Japanese officials?'

'It wasn't the officials. It was the computer. He charmed the computer.'

Rob wasn't really listening. He laughed and said, 'Have you seen my denim jacket?'

Rose shook her head. 'I suppose Marjorie used to pack for you.'

He looked at her in surprise. 'Well, she did as a matter of fact.'

'I've never done anyone's packing in my life.'

'And I don't expect you to start now! Come here.' Rob put his arms round her and kissed her neck. 'Marjorie never went anywhere with me,' he said. 'You're coming to Japan with me.'

'So is Andrew,' Rose said, not sounding very pleased about it.

3

Two have been caught. You are drawing them towards each other, towards you. They are on their way. But where are the others? Where? Where? Your awakening mind writhes with the agony of incompleteness. It calls. It reaches out.

You are in a dance studio in Adelaide, South Australia.

Look around.

The Contemporary Movement Group Studio is large and light, with high ceilings, wall mirrors and a black sprung floor.

There is music. Listen. Shakuhachi and koto whisper together in a rhythm that is familiar to you. It beats like a heartbeat, like blood through the veins you do not yet possess.

There are people here.

Look at the people.

A woman is standing by a cassette recorder. A group of teenagers, scattered across the floor, dance.

Look at the woman.

Shaz Christie is tall and so thin she looks almost two-dimensional. She is extremely flexible, with taut, whippy strength. Her black hair stands straight up from her bony forehead and is streaked with silver. She wears a silver nose ring and has a butterfly tattooed on her shoulder. She is not important.

Look at the dancers.

Elaine Taylor is a girl with spiky red hair and grey eyes. She is small and deceptively fine-boned. In fact she is strong and athletic and has great physical stamina. She is concentrating fiercely on the dance routine, moving to the unpredictable beat of the

Japanese music.

She is important.

Ben Challis is a boy with a sensitive face, light greenish eyes and fair hair, cut thick on top and shaved underneath. As he follows the movement—step, back, roll, leap, two steps forward, move it across—he mouths the words to himself. He is often self-conscious, but when he forgets that anyone is looking at him he is extraordinarily graceful.

He is important.

You do not recognise any of the other dancers. They are not important. But two of your cells are here. You remember them now. They penetrated your defences and unfroze your mind. They showed you your domain in its entirety.

The music grows and intensifies. You call out through it to them.

'I can take two of you,' Shaz Christie said when the rehearsal was over. 'That's all I've got funding for. Me and two others. The money'll cover airfares, and we'll stay with families so accommodation won't cost anything, but you'll have to bring money for meals and stuff like that. And Japan's very expensive. I'm broke and I won't be able to help you out much.'

She beat out a rapid rhythm on the small drum in front of her to punctuate her speech. 'It's in January—midwinter there and freezing. So you'll miss the summer and you'll have to take warmer clothes than you'd ever wear here. Anyone interested enough to take it further? I need to know this week so I can get cracking on visas and passports.'

Elaine's first reaction was swift and instinctive. *Yes. Take me!* Then she realised how unlikely it was she'd be able to go to Japan in January. She never had any money for a start, and her father, who loved travelling, would almost certainly want to get in the ute and drive to somewhere remote like Broome or the Bungle Bungles for the summer holidays.

Shaz was watching her carefully. 'I'd really like you to come, Elly. Do you think there's a chance you'd be able to?'

Elaine put her hand to her neck and fingered the silver medallion she always wore. She had started to shake her head when for a fraction of a second something happened to her mind. She frowned, and blinked, looking over her shoulder as though she could see something that shouldn't be there.

'Elly?' Shaz said again.

Elaine did not reply. She had a sudden flash of seeing herself as if she were in a movie. She saw herself dance in a way she knew she was capable of, but which she had never achieved so far. And someone was watching her ... someone she rarely dared to let herself think about any more ...

Still touching the medallion, she looked at Ben. Their eyes met. They both smiled slightly, a strange unearthly smile.

God, Shaz thought, watching them. There was something about these two that made them incredible together. And today they were more striking than ever. She had to take Elaine and Ben with her to Tokyo. They would be so receptive to new influences from Japanese dancers. It would make the show fantastic, quite unlike anything seen in youth arts before.

Ben had gone pale, his eyes huge with a force behind them that he didn't usually have. He needed that, Shaz thought, to give his performance strength as well as delicacy. He needed to discover something about himself and come to terms with it. She wondered briefly what it was: probably something to do with his sexuality. It usually was at fifteen if she remembered being that age correctly.

She should ask some of the other dancers if they wanted to go, she should be fair, but that wasn't really in her nature. She was more interested in excellence than fairness. She decided there and then that if she couldn't take Elaine and Ben with her she'd use the money for some other aspect of the production and go to Tokyo on her own. She rapped the drum furiously.

'So what do you two think?' she said impatiently. 'Any chance of it?'

'Sure,' Elaine replied. 'We'll come, won't we, Ben?'

'Wouldn't miss it for anything!'

'Great! I'll phone your parents tonight.'

'Yeah, phone them,' Ben said. 'It'll be cool. No problem.'

He and Elaine looked at each other again and grinned. There was something almost demonic about them.

'Fantastic!' Shaz said to herself.

4

You drift and dream. You wake again. The dreaming is shorter, the waking more intense. There are still cells missing. They are so far apart from each other and from you. You long for them, you search for them.

You are in the entrance hall of an apartment building in Osaka, Japan.

Look around.

A young man enters the building. He takes the elevator to the fifth floor, opens the door of Apartment 521 and goes in.

Look at the young man.

Toshihiro Toda is tall with thick, rather long black hair, and a handsome samurai face. Despite his impressive appearance, he has a gentle, almost timid nature, which he takes great care to hide under an impassive exterior. He is very intelligent and likes things to be done in the right fashion. He is meticulous. He is passionate about soccer, and likes Western music and films, but he is also very fond of traditional Japanese culture. He has a state-of-the-art PC on a low table and next to it an ink pad and writing brush. He practises jūdō five nights a week, and occasionally goes on retreats to temples to sit in zazen.

He is important.

Toshi threw his jacket and briefcase on the floor and went to his computer. Using the modem, he checked his e-mail. There were no messages for him. He picked up the phone and dialled a number. The phone rang and rang, but no one answered it. Even though he knew the number by heart, he took out his address book and checked again under 'I'.

'I' for Ito. The number was exactly as he'd dialled it. Just in case he'd dialled it wrong he tried again. Again there was no answer. It was strange. When he had dialled from E3, when the Australian, Mr Miller, had been there, he had left a message on the answer machine. But now even the machine didn't answer.

He buried his face in his hands, running his fingers through his silky hair. Then he tried a few more numbers—the bookshop, the library, the sushi bar on the corner, the Chinese restaurant where Ito ate at least once a week—each time asking politely if Professor Ito had been there, but he drew a complete blank. No one had seen the professor or his daughter for days.

Leonard Miller's visit had upset Toshi. Things were changing at E3. Everyone was tense and worried about the future. The heady days of the eighties, with full employment and huge economic growth, were over. Funding for research and development was dwindling. The managing director, Mr Kinoshita, had hinted that Headworld could make a very attractive takeover offer.

Everyone knew of Headworld's aggressive reputation. If they owned E3 Professor Ito would never be allowed to keep his games off the open market. Given the circumstances, his disappearance seemed very ominous. Why hadn't he confided in Toshi? Could someone have decided he should be taken out of the way?

The thought made Toshi extremely angry. He had been assigned to work with Professor Ito when E3 had offered to fund his research into new areas of electronic entertainment and virtual reality. It had been Toshi's first job, straight after graduating, and he had been filled with admiration for the professor's brilliant and quirky mind. And he had found in his boss something else, something rather similar to his own nature: a kind of optimistic idealism, an affectionate concern for young people, and a desire to make a better world for them.

Apart from Midori and the Australian children, Toshi had been the only person who had tested Space Demons and Skymaze. And if he had had his own way there would have been no others. He had strongly disapproved of involving any young people, let alone foreigners from a very different culture. But Professor Ito could be both stubborn and impulsive, and when his old friend Dr Hayford had asked if his computer whiz kid son Andrew could try one of the new games, he'd given Space Demons to him without considering the possible outcome.

Which had nearly been disastrous, Toshi remembered now. The Australian players had taken the games in a completely unexpected direction. It had been a marvellous example of chaos theory, in the professor's opinion. Just a few small changes at the start and things no one had dreamed of had developed.

Of course, Toshi had to agree, the whole experiment had been fascinating. There was no doubt the games were fantastic—far in advance of anything anyone else was doing at Nintendo, Fujitsu or even Headworld. Too fantastic, Toshi had thought all along, and lately the professor had seemed to be more in agreement with him. Work on the newest game, Shinkei, was progressing very slowly, and Ito was most reluctant to answer any enquiries about his work from the bosses at E3.

Now there were the rumours, compounded by the professor's disappearance. Toshi wondered if he should go to the police. But maybe Ito had gone into hiding. To start a search would be to endanger him further. Should he take his fears to the top people at E3? That was what a good worker should do. It would be the proper way to approach the problem. But if E3 were involved in Ito's disappearance, if they had had him murdered, they would not think twice about getting rid of Toshi too! And in the meantime, where was the latest game?

Toshi knew how dangerous the games were. He had to stop them being played or marketed by the wrong people.

Realising he was thinking in circles, he tried to get a grip on himself and calm his mind. He took off his office clothes—dark suit and white shirt—showered, and put on a blue-and-white–patterned yukata, with a quilted hanten over the top. He knelt on the floor in front of the low table, closed his eyes, breathed in and out deeply to centre himself, and took up the writing tools.

But on the second stroke of the letter his hand shook. The stroke went askew. There was someone outside the door. He heard muffled voices. The bell rang.

Toshi looked with disgust at the ruined page, crumpled it angrily and rose to his feet. He stepped off the tatami matting into his slippers, and opened the door.

Two men stood outside. Toshi had never seen them before but he recognised their type. It wasn't the type you wanted to have calling on you at nine o'clock on a winter's night—or at any other time. They were well rugged up in quilted parkas and caps, but he guessed that beneath their clothes their bodies would be colourfully tattooed in the yakuza fashion. The big one was the more immediately noticeable—a massive youth, like some of the boys Toshi competed with in the dōjō. He had a thick neck and close-cropped hair. With only a little bit more weight he'd make a sumō wrestler. But Toshi felt that the other man was more dangerous. The fat one was just a boy, and possibly stupid, but the older man had an expression of enraged intelligence in his eyes that Toshi didn't care for at all.

However, the men greeted him politely. The older man, who introduced himself as Yasunari, did most of the talking, in a Yokohama accent. The other, Tetsuo, sounded as if he came from a more rural area in the north.

'Forgive the rudeness, honourable sir. It's very late at night to be troubling you …'

Toshi didn't want to let them in, but neither did he want his neighbours in the building to be disturbed at this time of night. It made him smile inwardly at his upbringing. This was no time to be worrying about good manners and courtesy, but he couldn't help himself. The thought flashed into his mind that if these men had come to murder him he would probably die silently rather than disturb the neighbours.

'Sensei,' Yasunari interrupted his thoughts, using the respectful term even though he was almost certainly ten years older than Toshi. Perhaps he had noticed the calligraphy materials or perhaps he was impressed by Toshi's traditional attire. 'Would it be too much trouble to allow us inside?'

Tetsuo nodded his head several times in agreement with this request, and pushed forward.

'Dōzo, dōzo.' Toshi had no choice but to usher them in. Both men slipped off their cheap black shoes and stepped onto the tatami matting. They looked less threatening in their socks. Tetsuo even had a hole in one sock, through which Toshi could see a massive toe.

'Please, be seated.'

The two men ignored the Western-style chairs and knelt on the tatami. They both bowed formally to Toshi. He knelt and bowed back equally formally. He found the ritual calming but very faintly distasteful, with a touch of bushidō about it that always seemed to him (born in 1970) to have overtones of fascism. He wondered if he should offer tea, or beer. Sake would be more appropriate, but he didn't happen to have any.

'Toda sensei knows the reason for our visit?'

Toshi made a slight inclination with his head, indicating 'no'. He didn't think it was a good sign that they knew his name.

'We can perhaps receive from Toda sensei information as to the whereabouts of Professor Ito.'

Toshi said nothing for a few seconds. His face remained smooth and expressionless while his thoughts raced furiously. If these characters were looking for Ito it must mean he wasn't dead. But who had sent them? Miller? Kinoshita from E3? Or was it someone else who wanted to get their hands on the games?

'I'm afraid I cannot help you. Please excuse me. So sorry.'

'Cannot help or do not want to help?' Tetsuo grunted.

Yasunari held up a hand to silence him. 'Sensei must understand that we are very serious.'

Toshi understood this only too well. 'May I be told who wants to find him?'

Yasunari did not deign to answer this question, simply making a dismissive gesture.

'I cannot help you,' Toshi said again. 'I also would like to know where the professor is.'

Yasunari looked intently at him with his furious eyes. Then, abandoning his polite pose, he jumped with one swift, abrupt movement to his feet. 'We'll take a look around.'

Tetsuo got to his feet too with a suppleness that belied his great bulk. Probably trained in all the martial arts, Toshi thought ruefully to himself. He was opening his mouth to protest, more for the sake of form than because he thought it would make any difference, when something clicked in his mind. For a moment he wondered if fear hadn't brought on a sort of instant satori. He closed his eyes to examine what was going on in his brain.

He had made a connection with something he remembered and recognised—something which remembered and recognised him. He sat concentrating fiercely.

The two men watched him, impressed in spite of themselves. Then Yasunari gave the large youth a shove. 'Search the room!'

Toshi rose to his feet. A huge power was humming inside his head. He was no longer frightened. He wasn't even angry. He was simply irritated that these cockroaches were messing around in his belongings.

'Leave my house,' he said impatiently.

'Who do you think you're talking to?' Yasunari sneered.

Toshi made a sudden feint and Yasunari was on his back on the floor. A look of surprise crossed his face. He called to Tetsuo. 'Get him! Don't just stand there, you fool. You hold him while I search the room.'

Tetsuo held back. 'I don't know, boss. Don't you think we should go? Look at him. He's possessed by something. Look at his eyes.'

'You stupid potato! Don't give me that backblocks superstition. You're in the big city now. In the big time. Grab hold of him.'

As Tetsuo came warily towards him Toshi pointed at his foot. 'There's a hole in your sock!'

Tetsuo bent to look at it. Toshi caught him by surprise with a kick to the chin. The huge body came crashing down on top of Yasunari. With a strength he didn't know he possessed Toshi pulled him up by his coat collar. The coat and the shirt beneath it stretched open. At the base of his throat the young man had a circular tattoo of an eyeball with a blue teardrop where the pupil should be. Toshi recognised it with a shock. It was the symbol of Pure Mind—one of the secretive semi-religious groups that had been under investigation since the subway sarin gas attacks that had rocked Japanese society.

Toshi pushed the huge boy towards the door. Luckily he seemed quite cowed. Then Toshi bent over the older man and pulled open his shirt.

The same eye stared back at him.

'What does this mean?' he demanded. 'What does your organisation want with Professor Ito? Answer me!'

Yasunari got to his feet warily. Neither he nor Tetsuo took their eyes off Toshi. 'We were just told to find him,' he replied softly, holding his hands up placatingly. 'If you don't know where he is, that's fine, that's fine.'

'You only had to say so,' Tetsuo put in, rubbing his shoulder. Yasunari silenced him again.

'You should help us, sensei,' he said, again with a soft but dangerous tone to his voice. 'You like the old things, the old Japan, the way things used to be before we were corrupted by Western ideas.' He gestured towards the writing materials. 'That's all we want, all our Master wants. We want to keep Japan strong and beautiful and pure. Educated people like you and Professor Ito should join us. We are the future—your genius could be part of that.' He paused, his eyes never leaving Toshi's face. 'The computer programs...' he went on, casually. 'The Master is interested in them.'

Toshi couldn't help looking sceptical.

'True. As I said, we are the future. The Master believes in using the most modern technology to help us all follow the ancient paths of wisdom.'

'I think you should leave,' Toshi responded quietly. 'There is no way in which I can help you.'

The older man opened his mouth to speak again, but Toshi stared him down. He had no idea where the power was coming from, but there was something inside him which was making him invincible. 'Leave!' he ordered.

They bowed to him and backed down off the tatami, pulling on their shoes before going quietly out. Toshi closed the door carefully and bolted it from the inside. He went to the window and looked out at the darkened street. Lights from the apartment building opposite glowed with the illusion of safety. He saw his two visitors emerge from the lobby into the street. A third figure came out of the shadows and joined them. It was hard to see him clearly but his head appeared to be shaved and he was extremely thin. He wore overalls like a workman or technician and carried a tool bag. As he turned and bobbed his head deferentially to Yasunari, Toshi recognised him with a shock. Though his head was now shaved and he was much thinner, it was Ken'ichi Suzuki, an electronics technician who had been at E3 when Toshi had first arrived there. He had given notice six months later and Toshi had not seen him since. Now he looked as if he had become a fully fledged member of the Pure Mind movement.

The three men crossed the street and got into a car. Its engine started and it crawled away, its tail-lights gleaming redder on the corner.

Toshi turned back from the window, frowning. The visit had disturbed him immensely. He knelt again on the tatami and began to think very carefully, trying to understand and use the new power that had come into his mind.

5

'You can't just take off for Japan!' Mario Ferrone hadn't appeared to be listening to Ben and Elaine's excited conversation, but now he turned angrily from the screen.

'Why not?' Ben retorted. It was bad enough having Mario on his computer day and night without being bossed around by him in all details of his personal life.

'You could be happy for us,' Elaine said, giving Mario a friendly blow on the shoulder. 'But you're not the happy type really, are you? More brooding and—could it be—jealous?'

'Get stuffed!' Mario said without malice. He turned back to the screen and typed in a few words. He would never let her know but the thought of not seeing Elaine for four weeks depressed him enormously.

'Where are you now?' Ben said nervously, looking over his shoulder.

'In a very boring MUD. Talking to a very very boring wise person.'

'Don't you hate all those instant gurus? Everyone thinks they're so wise!' Ben said. He was jumpy with excitement and couldn't keep still. He made a tour of his parents' study where the three of them were exploring the Internet on the computer, stared out of the window at the brilliant summer day, made a leap to touch the wooden parrot that had hung from the ceiling ever since a trip to Tasmania six years before, and returned to stare at the screen again.

'Mm,' Mario mumbled in agreement. 'I think I'll leave and start again.'

'Where is this MUD?'

'It isn't anywhere, you dope. It's in cyberspace.'

Elaine made a trumpet with her hands and blew a mock fanfare.

'I'll see if I can find Skenvoy,' Mario said, his fingers flying over the keyboard.

'For someone who pretends to be illiterate, your typing's pretty nifty,' Elaine observed. Mario ignored her.

'So who the hell is Skenvoy? And where did you have to dial into?' Ben said. 'Is the phone bill going to cost the earth? What's my dad going to say when he gets a bill for thousands of dollars because you've been calling Los Angeles and Singapore and Amsterdam!'

'It won't cost that much. It's through this funny bulletin board you're on. It's only a local call. And Skenvoy is this really neat guy who turns up and makes comments on life. He's everywhere.'

'Not another instant guru?'

'Nah, Skenvoy's not a guru. Skenvoy's cool. Skenvoy embodies the true spirit of the Net. He's an anarchist.'

A menu of vaguely related subjects appeared on the screen. Mario ran his eyes over them rapidly. 'You know, you can learn about anything,' he said. 'All this information. All packed in together. Look at this! Military information, secret armies in the south-west of the United States, urban terrorism techniques, Pure Mind techniques.'

'What's Pure Mind?' Ben said.

'Nothing I'm interested in,' Mario said with a snigger. 'My mind is definitely not pure at all. It's probably some kind of sect. There are lots of them popping up. See, no one can really police or control the Net. So any organisation can use it for anything, send information anywhere in the world.' He moved on to another menu. 'Oh, here he is!'

Somewhere, Skenvoy said, *there exists the archetypal story. All over the world people are trying to write it, to compose it, to film it. But you all fall short. Your minds are human, finite, separate…*

'What's that mean?' Ben said after he'd read it twice.

'I'd have thought it was perfectly clear,' Mario replied.

'I know what the words mean,' Ben retorted. 'But what does it *mean*? What does it signify?'

'It doesn't signify anything,' Mario said. 'But when you read the next one, it'll be clearer. You can't explain Skenvoy. You either get it or you don't.'

Ben pulled a face at him.

'What am I going to do if you're away for four whole weeks?' Mario hit a key angrily. 'Not sure I can live without this stuff.'

'You're addicted to it,' Elaine said.

'You bet I am! It's so much fun!' Mario found it hard to explain how it felt to roam through cyberspace, a place which didn't really exist, but which seemed more real to him than the world he lived in. It was vast and full of power and he could be anyone he wanted to be. He could escape from his boring life of school and family and never having enough money to do anything, and not daring to think about the future, and what he would do when school ended. He wasn't at all sure he understood the procedure for living in the twenty-first century, but he understood life on the Net. The rules there, if there were any, made sense and you had to discover them for yourself—and you had all the lives you wanted. If you messed things up you could always start again next day or next week. And no one knew who you were, no one cared about your looks or your colour or your nationality or if you were two metres tall and had a stammer. He loved the chaotic sense of a world full of people who cared about their interests enough to chat endlessly about them. He loved the sense of communication, of talking to someone in Oslo or Thunder

Bay or Harare, and being able to disappear instantly from the conversation if it bored you to death.

As long as you could use a keyboard on the Net you were equal to anyone. And as long as you had access to a computer and a modem, of course.

'Can I still use the computer if you're in Japan?' he asked.

'That's all he's worried about,' Elaine said to Ben. 'He'll have to give up the superhighway for four weeks.'

'Four weeks is a hell of a long time. How come you get to go for four weeks? Who's paying for it?'

'Shaz arranged it all.'

'And you're allowed to go?'

'She's paying us, or at least someone's paying us. So that convinced everyone it was a brilliant idea!' Elaine still couldn't believe she was actually going to be allowed to do it. Of course, her father hadn't minded at all, the only problem was trying to keep him from formulating a plan to come with her. He'd never been to Japan and he was very taken with the thought of meditating in temples or studying martial arts. But now she had two lots of parents to deal with and Mrs Fields, who had been like her foster mother for the last year, had thought the trip was a very dangerous idea. She and her husband had a strange and one-eyed view of Japan, shared by many Australians of their generation who could never forget the horrors of the war.

When Elaine had tried to explain this to Shaz, the dancer had told her how much the Japanese people themselves had suffered in 1945 when Tokyo was almost totally destroyed and the atomic bombs were dropped on Hiroshima and Nagasaki.

'No one country has a monopoly of cruelty,' she said. 'It's inside us all, and the more we deny that dark side the more likely it is to explode out of control sooner or later.'

Elaine knew this was true—she'd seen it happen herself

in the computer games she'd played with Andrew Hayford, Ben and Mario. She trusted Shaz because Shaz never tried to pretend that the dark side didn't exist, unlike Mrs Fields, who kept it firmly at bay with niceness and kindness.

Niceness and kindness were great qualities and Elaine wasn't knocking them at all, but if you didn't recognise the dark side then how could you face it and deal with it?

In her dance classes Shaz led her students forward through the darkness, like going through the Dark Clouds that Elaine had had to overcome in Skymaze, and going forwards made her feel strong and safe. She fingered the medallion that had been her reward for solving Skymaze. She couldn't stop thinking about the computer games lately. 'It must be because I'm going to Japan where they came from,' she told herself.

'Didn't your parents object though?' she said to Ben. 'They were quite suspicious of Shaz when you first joined the group weren't they?'

'It was strange,' Ben admitted. 'It was as if they really didn't want me to go, but they couldn't help themselves. They had to say yes!'

'Some supernatural power is leading you to Japan,' Mario intoned dramatically.

'What makes you say that?' Ben asked.

Mario looked up at him from the screen in surprise. 'I don't know. Why? Is it true?'

'It's just … it's all been so easy!'

'Yeah,' Elaine said. 'Does make you wonder, doesn't it?'

She and Ben looked at each other and laughed. 'I'm so excited,' she said.

'Me too!'

'What about me?' Mario complained. 'What am I going to do all summer when everyone's away? Whose computer am I going to use?'

'What about Andrew's? He'll be back soon, won't he?'

Mario stared at Ben. 'Don't tell me you don't know?'

'What?'

'Andrew's gone to Japan with his father.'

'You're kidding! I thought he was coming back from Sydney after New Year.'

'No, he phoned me from Sydney and said he was going to Tokyo and he was going to see the crazy professor.'

'Professor Ito?'

'Our man in Osaka himself! Except he's not in Osaka any more, apparently. So they're going to meet him in Tokyo.'

'That's extraordinary,' Ben said. 'We're going to be in Tokyo at the same time!'

'Like I said.' Mario returned to the keyboard. 'There's some supernatural force drawing you all together.' After a few moments of idle typing he went on, 'But why isn't it drawing me together too?'

'It's pure coincidence,' Elaine said.

Ben agreed. 'Masses of people go to Japan in the summer holidays. My mum was talking to someone in a souvenir shop and she said dozens of schools are sending exchange groups and so on. The whole place is going to be swarming with Australians.'

'It'll be winter there though,' Elaine said. 'Do you think it'll snow?'

'Bound to,' Ben replied.

'I've never seen snow,' she said. 'Have you?'

'Dad took us to ski one year at Mount Hotham.'

Mario made a groaning noise.

Elaine looked at him closely. 'Turn round,' she said. 'I want to see your face.'

'Get lost,' he said, resisting her hands on his neck.

'You are jealous, aren't you?'

'I'd love to go to Japan,' he admitted. 'And I'd love to meet Professor Ito.'

Elaine was so excited and happy she felt more than usually generous. 'Here,' she said, taking the medallion from round her neck. 'You can have this while I'm away. Remind you of the Skymaze. And me!'

'Why would I want to be reminded of someone who looks like a red-haired grasshopper?' Mario replied, but he took the medallion almost eagerly, and looked at it, smiling.

'Well, say thank you!' Elaine prompted him.

'Thanks!' He put the medallion in his pocket. But it didn't really make him feel any less like the one on the outside, always left out of the main action. He looked back at the screen.

If your minds could be linked, Skenvoy said, *if the story wrote itself accommodating your wildest desires and responding to your deepest fears...*

'What a load of rubbish,' Ben said cheerfully. 'Go somewhere else.'

Mario quit and set the modem to redial. Nothing happened for a few moments.

Look around.

You are in a house in Adelaide, South Australia. The house is surrounded by trees. Beyond the trees are suburbs and beyond them the silvery shine of the sea.

Look at the room.

A study. Bookshelves, filing cabinets, two desks, phone, answer machine, fax, computer.

There are three people in the room.

Look at the people.

They are all important. Two of them you have already summoned. They are on their way. You are drawing them towards you.

The third? He is part of you as well. He needs to be summoned to be part of the whole. But he is already keyed in to some source of energy. You approach and look through his eyes.

You reel, bewildered and amazed. More power than you ever dreamed of, realms that you could not have imagined. You are just a child compared to this. You thought you were all-powerful, but you have come face to face with mature and adult power. You see that you are only an infant. You rage.

'Wow!' Mario exclaimed in astonishment.

'What is it?' Ben leaned over his shoulder and peered into the screen.

'It was, like, really slow to get into, and then it suddenly went zap! And look how fast it's moving now!'

The type was unscrolling at such a rate the words were lost in a blur.

'Damn!' Mario muttered, clicking the mouse and pressing keys at random. 'How d'you control the speed, Ben?'

'I don't know! It's never done that before! You've broken it.'

'I didn't do anything!'

'Dad's going to kill me!' Ben groaned.

The screen abruptly went black, making a sound that seemed to echo Ben's groan.

The three of them stared at each other.

'Something very peculiar is going on,' Ben said.

The doorbell rang, making them jump. When Ben opened the door, Mario's brother John was standing there, face red and sweaty from the long bike ride up the hill.

'Hey,' he said. 'Is your phone bust? I've been trying to call you and it's always busy. Is Mars here?'

'You can blame him for the phone,' Ben said. 'He's been on the Net all afternoon.'

John made a face and pushed past him. 'Mars,' he shouted. 'You've got to come home.'

Mario did not reply for a moment or two. He was still staring at the darkened screen. Then he breathed out, and stretched his arms over his head. 'Oh well, looks like the computer's stuffed anyway.'

Ben was fiddling with the mouse, trying to get some response from the screen. He switched the modem off and the phone immediately began ringing.

'Geez, it's probably my parents!'

'Gotta go,' Mario said. 'See you later.' At the door he turned and said, 'Do you reckon you could ask if I can come round while you're away, and use the computer some more?'

'You must be joking! I'm going to have a hard enough time explaining how you wrecked it.'

'I'd better go too,' Elaine said. 'Don't want to desert you and all that, but I've got to pack.'

'Let yourselves out,' Ben said, picking up the phone.

As he sighed, 'Hi, Mum,' he glanced towards the computer. A light pulsed briefly on the screen and it emitted another curious sound, almost like a baby gurgling.

Inside his brain something responded. It was so slight he was only partly aware of it. Then he tried to pacify his mother who was having minor hysterics on the other end of the phone.

6

At first Andrew thought he was imagining it all. Then he realised there was something he did with his mind, a little trick of concentrating and focusing—and things worked out in his favour. Once it had always been like that. While he was still at primary school he really did believe that the universe was organised entirely for his benefit. But his parents' separation and divorce, his mother's remarriage—which had meant the acquisition of his obnoxious stepbrother, Paul—and going to high school had given this belief rather a knock.

Now it seemed his life was back on track. The old Hayford charm must be working again. It made him feel happy and confident, the way he used to feel when he was eleven. Only occasionally did he feel uneasy, as though something else were working out his life for him.

He had been really looking forward to meeting Professor Ito. It felt as if that were the whole point of his trip to Japan. So he was disappointed when, after a perfect flight from Sydney, he, his father and Rose arrived at Narita International Airport to find they were met by no one.

'This is very strange,' Rob said after another fruitless search of the huge arrivals area. 'Ito's usually so punctilious. I hope he hasn't had an accident.'

Rose was leaning on the luggage trolley looking exhausted. 'Are you sure he knew we were coming? Maybe all those changes of plan confused him.' She looked at Andrew, who was staring fixedly into space as though he could summon Ito up by magic.

'We spoke just after Christmas,' Rob replied. 'That was when he suggested we change the flight to Narita rather than go straight to Osaka. He wanted us to stay in Tokyo for a few days so he could show us around. And it was school holidays so his daughter would be with him—he distinctly mentioned that, because I've never met her.'

'Did you tell him I was coming?' Andrew asked.

'No, that all happened in such a rush, I haven't spoken to him since we arranged it,' Rob said, peering at each passing Japanese person in case he might have forgotten what Professor Ito looked like.

'We've got the hotel booking, haven't we?' Rose interrupted him.

'Yes, it's the Hilton. I've stayed there before. It's very nice.'

Rose shrugged. 'We'd better just go to the hotel and try and phone him from there.'

As they made their way to the Tokyo shuttle Andrew felt a terrible sense of loss. He felt as if he were heading in the wrong direction. He staggered a little, quite dizzy. 'Must be the flight,' he thought. 'And I was so looking forward to seeing old Ito.'

'You all right, Andrew?' his father asked.

'Bit fed up, actually.'

'Don't take it personally!' his father replied. 'Professor Ito didn't even know you were coming.'

'Tokyo will be really exciting,' Rose said, as though she herself had expressly arranged for this great metropolis to come into being for their entertainment.

Rob also tried to cheer him up. 'Look at the automatic machines, Andrew. I love 'em. You hungry or thirsty? You can get all sorts of drinks—hot or cold. Hot tea or coffee in a can!'

Andrew scowled at the machine. His mind went blank for a second. Then he saw himself, a white-clad figure, on a snowy mountain...He looked into his own eyes and saw his own power...

The machine gave a sort of electronic howl, and spat all its cans out at once. They cascaded onto the terrazzo floor and rolled in every direction. People tripped. Trolleys skidded. Airport officials came running.

Andrew surveyed the chaos in amazement. 'Geez, I think I did that,' he muttered.

Luckily no one heard him. And for the rest of the journey he took great care not to look or scowl at anything.

In the hotel they had adjoining rooms. Rose said she was rather disappointed not to be staying somewhere more typically Japanese, but Andrew already felt disoriented enough. He was relieved to find the hotel quite familiarly Western.

He switched on the TV in his bedroom and stared at it moodily. There was some extraordinary game show on. The compère yelled at the top of his voice and at the rate of about a hundred words a second. A team of young men were humiliating each other with baseball bats and bags of flour. Despite a year of learning Japanese at school Andrew couldn't understand anything. Now and then he caught a fragment of a word he knew: *desu, gozaimasu, sumimasen*.

He switched the TV off and went into Rob and Rose's room. Rob was holding the phone to his ear, not speaking. He shook his head and put the phone down. 'No answer. What can have happened to him?'

He sat heavily down on the bed and stared at the TV, where the same game show was on. 'I'll never understand them,' he muttered. 'They're all completely mad!'

Rose went past on her way to the bathroom. She tapped him on the arm playfully. 'Don't generalise. Imagine what Japanese visitors to Australia think of "Sale of the Century" or "Perfect Match".'

'I never watch them,' Rob retorted.

'Well, there you are. I bet your friend Professor Ito doesn't watch this stuff either. If we judged countries by their TV programs we'd all give up on the human race entirely!'

'I just don't understand Masa letting us down like that,' Rob said grumpily. 'I thought he was a real friend. I guess I got it wrong.'

'Don't be silly,' Rose said. 'You're just tired from travelling. That's what's put you in a bad mood. Go for a walk or something. I'm going to have a shower.'

Rob stared at the TV for a few more seconds and then got to his feet. 'I'm going down to the bar,' he called through the bathroom door. 'You want to join me there?'

'Sure!' Rose called back above the running water.

'Andy?'

Andrew shrugged. He didn't really reel like doing anything. He was tired after the trip, but he also felt extremely restless. 'I'll stay here,' he said. 'Maybe they'll call.'

Rob left the room. Andrew heard the hum of the elevator from down the corridor. Rose was singing in the bathroom. The door was still half open and steam escaped into the room, giving it a mysterious, theatrical atmosphere.

The phone rang.

Andrew leaped across the room and picked it up.

'May I speak with Dr Hayford, please?' It was a man's voice, the English perfect, with a very slight Japanese accent.

'He's just gone down to the bar. Is that Professor Ito?'

There was silence on the other end of the line. Then the professor (Andrew was sure it was him) said, 'Is that Dr Hayford's son? Andrew?' Without giving Andrew time to reply, the voice went on, 'But what are *you* doing in Tokyo? This is very unexpected.'

'I was hoping to see you,' Andrew replied. 'We were very

disappointed you didn't turn up. Is everything all right?'

'I am very sorry. It was most impolite of me. I am unable to meet you at the moment. Maybe I can phone next week.'

'What's going on?' Andrew demanded.

'I cannot speak over the phone. I must go now. Please give my most sincere regards to your father...'

'Is it something to do with the games?' Andrew interrupted impatiently.

'Why do you say that?' The voice went up several levels in anxiety. 'You mustn't mention the games to anyone.'

'Why not? Is there a new one? Did you get our letter? We finished Skymaze. It turned into a... Hello! Hello!'

The line had gone dead.

'Damn!' Andrew muttered.

Rose yelled from the bathroom, 'Andrew, can you pass me one of those robes on the bed?'

'Okay.' He picked up one of the Japanese-style dressing gowns and went to the bathroom door. Rose was wrapped in a towel, with another one round her head. She took the robe. 'Thanks. Were you talking to someone?'

'Phone,' he said, trying to avoid looking at her bare skin. 'It was Professor Ito.'

'Oh good! He hadn't just abandoned us then! What happened to him?'

'He didn't say. Just that he was very, very sorry.'

'Did he leave his number?'

'No.'

'Oh!' Rose looked pensive for a few seconds, then shrugged, gave Andrew a smile and closed the door in his face.

Andrew took a can of cola from the mini-bar fridge and went back to his room. The can was tiny—a sort of miniature Japanese version of Coke. It added to his sense that the world was out of kilter.

7

Each cell brings more awareness. But increased awareness also increases the pain of separation. Your brain is growing like a baby's in the womb. Each cell activates more of you. Soon you will have your birth.

You are in a house near Itako, in Ibaraki prefecture, Japan.

Look at the house.

The house is in the old Japanese style. It has a sloping tiled roof with curved gables and eaves. Inside it is furnished in the traditional manner, with sliding doors, screens and tatami matting. In the kitchen an old woman is preparing breakfast.

Look at the woman.

Etsuko Ito is seventy years old. Her face is wrinkled but her hair is still black. She is very small, and slightly bent, mainly because she didn't get enough to eat during her teenage years, which coincided with the Second World War. She is wearing quilted trousers and several sweaters against the extreme cold of the house. Over the sweaters she wears an apron. She is cutting up vegetables to make miso soup for breakfast. Rice is cooking in an electric rice cooker, and the coffee maker is dripping coffee.

She is not important.

Look through the house. In another room a teenage girl is asleep on the floor.

Look at the girl.

Midori Ito looks fierce even when she is asleep. Her mouth is slightly open. She turns energetically in her sleep and grinds her teeth. Her long black hair is all over her face.

She is important. She has already been called. Now she must be drawn to meet the others.

There is no one else in the house, but behind the house and across a small garden is a stone storeroom.

Look in the storeroom.

The storeroom is filled with boxes, trunks and lacquer chests. Down one side a space has been cleared on top of a wide shelf and a man is working here on two desktop machines. Extension cords run haphazardly from the only power point near the door.

The man is working furiously on the computer. A cup of coffee stands on the bench beside him.

Look at the man.

It is Masahiro Ito.

It is not clear to you if he is important or not. He is not a cell like the others you have called, but you know he has played a part in your creation. A word floats into your embryonic mind, a word you did not know you knew.

Otōsan.

Father!

Midori was woken up by sparrows chattering and squabbling in the persimmon tree outside the window. Her grandmother had slept next to her but the futon on the floor was now empty, the quilts pushed neatly back. Midori snuggled down under her own quilts and grinned. Usually obāsan would have packed the bedding away in the big cupboard as soon as she got up. It was nice of her to leave her granddaughter to sleep in a little longer.

It was nice to be here, even though she missed her friends in Osaka. She wondered what Keiko and Michiko would be doing. Well, probably nothing so very different from her since it was so soon after Oshōgatsu—New Year's Day. They'd be visiting relatives and receiving otoshidama—gifts of money— far more than she had received, probably, especially Keiko whose family were so rich!

Not that it mattered. She had no way of spending money here. They were miles away from the nearest shopping centre, and her father didn't want to take her out anywhere, and her grandmother had never learnt to drive. It was a mystery to Midori how obāsan survived in the old family house on her own, but there were always people coming to the door, keeping an eye on her, delivering food or offering to drive her to Itako or Kashima Jingū. Neighbours came to drink tea and chat. It was so distant from Midori's life in Osaka in time as well as in space.

She liked being here, but she couldn't help wondering when they would be going back. School would be starting again in a few days. But her father hadn't mentioned returning. In fact he hadn't really mentioned anything since they had been at grandmother's. He'd just worked day and night on the computer. At least Midori had had plenty of time to finish her physics assignment as well as doing all the revision she'd planned and more. It would be a very pleasant surprise for her teachers.

Her father refused to go out anywhere, wouldn't talk to any of her grandmother's visitors even though they'd all known him from childhood, wouldn't even answer the phone. Obāsan was instructed to tell people vaguely that he wasn't there, almost as if they were in hiding. What a ridiculous idea! It was impossible to go into hiding in Japan, despite the millions of people living there. Everyone always knew where you were and what you were up to, and if they didn't, they made it their business to find out.

She lay on the futon, listening to the sparrows, and enjoying the luxurious warmth of the quilts. She really didn't want to get up, because the house would be so cold, but she could smell breakfast, and anyway, she felt she had to go and see

how her father was getting on with his plan to bring the game
Shinkei back under control.

'He can't control it,' something said inside her mind. 'It's
already out of control.' The thought was both alarming and
exciting. She put her hand up to her neck and felt for the medallion, then remembered she had tucked it under the futon
the night before. She took it out and looked at it. As always
it reminded her of Toshi. She wondered if he was worrying
about them, if he would try to find them. She felt awful about
leaving without telling him. She wished she could at least
phone him. She remembered the man she'd seen outside the
apartment the night they'd left Osaka. Was it really possible
he had been tapping their phone? Out here in the country
it all seemed so unlikely. She closed her eyes and thought of
Toshi, imagined he was in the room with her.

Something altered in the room. Her eyes snapped open.
For an instant she thought she saw Toshi there. Then she
knew with complete certainty that though he wasn't there yet
he soon would be. He was going to come and find her.

Was that good or bad? Oh, good, surely! She so much wanted to see him. But would her father want to see Toshi? Or was
he hiding from him too?

It would be all right. She would make it all right. She felt
she could do anything she wanted to. She dropped the medallion on the floor and pushed back the quilts. Aaah, the room
was freezing. She threw on her clothes.

She was too excited to eat breakfast, so she went straight
to the sliding door that led into the garden and, putting the
startled sparrows to flight, ran across to the storeroom. She
rapped impatiently on the door.

'You look terrible,' she said to her father when he opened it.

'Midori-chan, what are you doing up so early?'

'What about you?' she returned. 'Or didn't you go to bed?'

Her breath hung on the frosty air.

His face was serious. 'Come inside. It's not much warmer in here but it is a little. And I need to talk to you.'

'How's it going?' she asked as she stepped inside.

'The master software has gone maverick,' he replied. 'It's not responding at all. It's taking on a life and will of its own. Of course, it was very close to real intelligence ...' He fell silent, shaking his head in unwilling admiration of what he had created. Then he went on with his explanation. 'Normally when you play a computer game you may improve, become more skilful, faster and so on, but the software stays the same. It's incapable of improvement. But the complexity of the games we created seems to have led to some sort of interaction. The program has changed in some way, using the players. Almost as if it's become organic.'

He sat down in front of one of the machines and clicked the mouse. Midori recognised the faces that came up on the screen, even though she had never met them. She read the names under each picture: *Andrew Hayford, Ben Challis, Elaine Taylor, Mario Ferrone.* And then came her own picture and name, followed by Toshi's.

'These are the players. I think the program may be trying to draw them all together.'

'How do you know?' Midori asked slowly.

'I phoned Dr Hayford last night. I didn't feel it was safe to meet him at Narita, and anyway, my first priority must be to disarm the program before anything irrevocable happens. But I have never done anything so ill-mannered in my life. What will he think of me? Such an old and valued friend. I couldn't bear the thought of him waiting and waiting for me at the airport. So I called the hotel to apologise.'

He stopped and seemed to be deep in thought.

'Well,' Midori prompted him.

'Dr Hayford's son answered the phone,' her father continued. 'Andrew Hayford is in Tokyo!'

'His father probably decided to bring him for a holiday,' she replied. 'It's not so strange.'

'But look at this!' Her father picked up the morning newspaper, the *Mainichi Yomiuri*. It was opened on the arts page. Midori read, *Youth Arts Festival attracts international talent*. Below the headline was a photo of three Westerners—a very tall black-haired woman and two teenagers.

'Elaine Taylor and Ben Challis,' Professor Ito said. 'Three of the Australian players have arrived here. Is that a coincidence or is it something more sinister?'

When Midori didn't answer, he looked closely at her. 'Tell me honestly, has anything strange happened to your mind? Is something trying to make contact with you, take you over?'

'Maybe,' she said, and then immediately, 'No!'

Her father put his head in his hands and groaned. 'I've created a monster! If these young Australians are being drawn here, who else will be looking for them? Apart from the dangers of the game—and I've no way of discovering what they are—suppose Headworld and E3 are also aware of the importance of the players to the game?'

Midori studied him dispassionately. She'd never seen her clever father so distraught. She realised she wasn't as distressed as she should have been. Perhaps something was influencing her mind. She ran her eyes round the room, and then went to the tiny peephole by the door and looked out. She was seeing things in just the same way as she did normally, except she kept feeling Toshi was nearby. And then she saw a flash, like a film clip, of herself, walking into a Tokyo hotel.

She walked into a hotel. It was the Hilton.
She walked into a hotel. It was the Hilton.
She walked into ...

Midori shook herself. 'Strange,' she muttered. She turned back to her father. 'Are the Hayford family staying at the Hilton?'

'Did I tell you that?'

She'd always shared everything with her father but now she felt secretive. 'I guess so,' she said and then went on casually, 'How much longer are we staying here? I've got to think about school.'

'Haven't you taken in anything I've said? Don't you understand what a crisis this is?' He was almost shouting at her. 'We can't make any plans until I've put things right, and that's got to be before E3 or Headworld catch up with me.'

'Calm down, Dad,' she said, infuriatingly. 'Everything's going to be fine. I just want to know when I'll be back at school, because I've got exams right after term starts.' She stared at him. She was making plans that had nothing to do with school or exams.

The rice paddies were white with frost as Midori pedalled down the road on obāsan's old bicycle which she'd found in the yard under a plastic sheet. There was a train to Tokyo from Itako in an hour and a half. She should make it easily.

She felt awful about deceiving her father and her grandmother. It was the first time she'd ever done anything like that. She'd told them she was just going out for a ride and would be back in a couple of hours. By the time she was on the train they'd be starting to worry, but she'd phone them from Tokyo. Luckily she still had all her New Year's money so she wasn't short of cash.

She wasn't really quite sure what she was doing, or if it was the right thing to do, but she had the strongest compulsion that she had to start finding the others. Three of them were already in Tokyo. So she had to go to Tokyo too. She knew where Andrew was, so she would start with him. She would go to the Hilton.

She got a seat easily at Itako, but by the time the limited express drew into Tokyo station it was packed with Sunday travellers visiting family or going in to the capital to go to the theatre or to concerts—women in traditional kimono, men in suits, mothers carrying babies inside their ombu coats, young couples on their way to Disneyland or Harajuko. Midori followed the crowd, hoping she wouldn't get lost. She'd only been to Tokyo a few times before in her life. She took out her railway guide to check the platform she had to find next.

The Hilton was near Shinjuku station, so she had to take the Yamanote loop, which was one of the few JR lines she knew about. She had to follow the green signs. At last she found the right platform and got on the train.

'Midori-chan!' Professor Ito called out to his daughter as he stepped up into the house at midday. He had got no further with his work on the program, but he needed a break and some food.

His mother came out of the kitchen where she had been making rice cakes. 'She went to Tokyo!'

'What?'

'I thought you must have known. One of the neighbours saw her cycling to Itako and then the yaki imo man told me he saw her getting on the train. You want some imo? I bought some pieces, I know how much Midori loves it.'

'No,' he said. The smell of the sweet potato made him feel slightly sick. He shook his head in despair. How could he hope to hide anywhere? Everyone always knew what everyone else was doing. And if the neighbours and the yaki imo man knew Midori had gone to Tokyo, who else might know? Who else might be following her even now?

Had she gone to find the other players? Was she acting of her own free will or was something else driving her? Were his suspicions right and was some force bringing all the players together for a game over which he no longer had any control? A game which was programming itself, and which would soon start playing itself?

'Fancy little Midori-chan going to Tokyo all by herself,' his mother was saying. 'I expect she's meeting friends, ne?'

'Of course,' he replied shortly. 'There's nothing to worry about.' But he was sick with worry. He had no idea what to do now. He phoned Dr Hayford at the Hilton only to be told the phone was off the hook and that the hotel was not in the habit of giving out information on its guests and their visitors. He felt he should rush off to Tokyo to look for his daughter, but even if he started at the Hilton, how would he know where to go from there? Midori could be anywhere in a metropolis of fourteen million people.

His only hope was to control the game before it went completely beyond him. He asked his mother to make him fresh coffee and went back to the storeroom. He gazed at the faces on the computer screen.

'Where are you all now?' he said aloud. 'And what is happening to you?'

8

South Australia lay baking in the grip of El Niño, land drying to dust, trees desiccated. In the city and suburbs sprinklers kept gardens green and trees alive, but, with water restrictions looming, more and more people were giving up their gardens in despair.

The Ferrones weren't among them. Every evening after work Lina Ferrone was out in the garden, watering the fruit trees, the vegetable garden and the flowers round the front. But this evening, when Mario and John returned from a trip to the swimming pool, there was no sign of their mother in the garden. The house had a subdued, almost funereal air to it when they went inside. It made them feel very uneasy.

They backed out and had the usual argument about who should hang up the towels. John lost and went to put them on the Hills hoist beyond the fruit trees, and Mario opened the screen door again warily. He couldn't think of anything he'd done wrong, but this sort of atmosphere usually meant that a storm was about to break over his head.

He thought he'd been keeping out of trouble lately—even though he was bored out of his brain. So bored he'd even let John talk him into going to the pool, and had then spent almost all afternoon there, chasing and ducking John (and being ducked by him) and jumping off the spring board with a whole bunch of kids to see who could make the biggest splash.

Now, his eyes red from chlorine and his skin both waterlogged and sunburnt, he felt like heading straight for the shower and then eating a huge meal. After that it would be great to spend the night on the Net, but there was no chance of that with no computer in the house. The thought occurred to him that Ben's parents might have complained to his father about the computer that had mysteriously seized up. Well, no one could prove it was his fault, and anyway, Ben's older brother Darren, the self-styled super hacker, must have got it going by now.

He thought reluctantly about computers, wondered what cryptic messages Skenvoy had been relaying, wished he could get back on the Net.

He was about to dash into the shower to beat John to it, when his mother came out of the kitchen. Her face was pale and her eyes red.

'Mario,' she said, 'call John and come into the kitchen. We need to talk to you.'

Mario went to the back door and yelled for John. His brother was at the end of the yard, eating apricots off the tree. He turned and waved to show he'd be there in a minute. Mario went back into the house.

Aldo, his father, was sitting at the kitchen table. It was very unusual for him to be home from work so early.

'What's up?' Mario said.

His father turned and looked him up and down. 'How old are you, son?'

'You know how old I am! I'm nearly sixteen.'

'Sixteen in June,' his mother reminded him. 'That's six months away.'

'Five months, Mum. So I'm more than fifteen and a half.'

His mother spoke in Italian to his father. Mario often pretended not to understand them, but in fact he knew perfectly well what they were saying, and could have spoken to them in the same language if he'd wanted to.

'He's too young to leave for so long.'

'He should be old enough. He should be acting like a man.'

'Things are different here. The young grow up slower.'

'When I was his age I was responsible. He should be taking responsibility. Anyway, Franco can come and stay in the house. What problem can there be?'

'You know, dear, Franco and Mario—they irritate each other.'

'Then they can learn not to!' His father added one of his elaborate swear-words. Mario decided it was time to interrupt.

'What's going on?' he said. 'And what's Frank got to do with it?'

'Your grandmother is very sick,' his mother said, her voice breaking into a half sob. His father reached out and patted her clumsily on the hand. There were tears in his eyes too. 'She wants to see us. She's afraid she is going to die.'

'She's very strong,' Aldo said. 'I don't think she's likely to die.'

Lina gave him a tender but frustrated look, 'She's eighty, tesoro. Old people die. And we should be there. We need to say goodbye, and then afterwards help arrange things.' She got up from the table, grabbed a tea-towel and wiped her eyes. Speaking quickly to Mario she said, 'Your father and I feel we should both go back to Alberobello. It means leaving you and John for the holidays.'

'That's cool,' Mario said. 'I can look after things here.'

'You'll have to do your bit,' Aldo said. 'But Frank is going to come back for a few weeks, keep an eye on you.'

'Does he have to? We'll be fine on our own.'

'Don't be silly, son,' his mother said. 'You and John are too young to leave alone. I'll be worried enough with Frank here.' She approached Mario and held him by the shoulders, looking seriously into his face. He was taller than she was and she had to look up. 'You will be good? You must promise me.'

John came into the kitchen, his face sticky with apricot juice. The rich smell of the fruit hung around him. The kitchen faced west and the setting sun threw shadows from the vine outside in leaf patterns on the floor.

'They're going away,' Mario said. 'Back to Italy. Nonna's ill. Frank's coming back to look after us.'

John's face fell. 'What about going to Port Hughes, Dad? You were going to take us fishing this year!' He looked from his mother to his father and back again. His face crumpled. He went and put his arms round his mother. 'Nonna's not going to die, is she?'

His mother patted him on the back. 'Don't cry, Johnny, don't cry, son. You must be a brave boy for Mamma, okay? And help Frank look after the house, and the garden. And the chooks.'

'And Mario,' their father added with feeling.

'It's going to be such a boring summer,' Mario said, sitting down at the table, opposite his father.

'You'll miss us, darling?' His mother had gone to the stove and was starting to cook dinner. Fresh vegetables from the garden lay on the bench: zucchini, eggplant and tomatoes, together with basil and oregano from the pots of herbs that stood round the back door. The bruised smell of basil filled the kitchen. Mario suddenly knew that for the rest of his life that smell would remind him of this moment and of his mother.

'I suppose I will,' he said.

Lina turned and smiled at her husband over Mario's shoulder. 'One thing might make you happier. Tell him, Aldo.'

'I hope it'll keep him out of trouble,' his father grunted.

'What?' Mario suddenly had the most peculiar feeling, as if his life were a jigsaw and a piece of great importance was about to slip into place.

'Frank's engineering firm got him into this computer stuff,

what's it called, Lina?'

'CAD.'

'Whatever that stands for! Anyway, he's bought this fancy new computer and he's bringing it here when he comes to stay.'

'Remember Dr Freeman said you should be encouraged in your computer interests?' his mother said. 'Well, Frank says you can use it in the evening, as long as you're careful. And he can teach you a lot about it too. Not just playing games, but programming and everything.'

'I guess it would have a modem,' Mario said slowly. 'Does that mean I can go on the Net?'

'Whatever, darling. We just want you to have something to do while we're away.'

'Me too?' said John. 'Can I go on it too?'

His mother smiled indulgently at him. 'Of course you can.' But her husband interrupted her. 'This is for Mario. Let him have one thing in his life that he doesn't have to share with John.'

Mario was amazed. He couldn't believe what he was hearing. 'Thanks,' he said awkwardly.

'Just don't stuff things up.' Rather to Mario's relief his father reverted to his normal self.

'That's not fair,' John wailed.

'Don't whinge,' Mario told him. 'I expect we'll let you have a turn on it.'

Later that night, lying in bed, he thought of Elaine and Ben and wondered what they were getting up to in Japan. He mused on the new and unexpected turn of events. For the first time in his life he felt as if he were in control. Things were working out in his favour. Then he remembered his grandmother and felt a little guilty. He didn't really want her to be sick. But if she hadn't been sick his parents wouldn't have decided to go away and he wouldn't have got access to Frank's computer. He flexed his mind slightly, and felt a new power, something he had never really experienced before—but it reminded him of the way he'd felt in the game Skymaze when he'd decided to go back into the maze and had rescued his friends. He felt as if he could make choices that were profound and heroic. He fell asleep, smiling.

9

'Wow!' Shaz said. 'This is really elegant!'

Elaine looked rather nervously around the theatre. They were in a place called the National Children's Castle in Shibuya, but how they'd got there from where they were staying with Shaz's friend Haruko, she had no idea. They had been in Japan for two days and she was suffering from severe culture shock.

Not that it was really unpleasant. It was exciting and stimulating, and she loved everything she'd seen—the way Tokyo, at first sight a vast and unwelcoming city of steel and concrete, suddenly revealed itself to be a mass of little villages, each one fascinating; the wonderful variety of goods in the stores and supermarkets; the way you could be in the middle of a fashion department and see an old tailor working on an exquisite kimono; the delicious food at the cheap noodle shops they'd eaten in; the masses of cheerful, well-dressed people. There were some bad parts too—the press of commuters on the trains during rush hour, the Japanese-style toilets which she wasn't sure she'd ever get used to, the homeless people moving their cardboard boxes into position in the subways every afternoon as the day grew colder. Really the subways were full of horror, especially if one kept thinking about sarin gas attacks and earthquakes.

The worst thing was not being able to read street signs and shop signs, and not being able to understand anything people said around her. It was the first time she'd been out of Australia and it was a revelation to her. Her country wasn't the centre of the world after all! If the world had a centre, it was surely here in this vast and powerful city with its clever and energetic people. She wished she'd learnt some Japanese, but it wasn't taught at Fernleigh High School.

'What do you think, Elly?' Shaz's voice interrupted her thoughts.

'It's great,' she said, looking at the round theatre with its striking black-and-white decor and ultra-modern staging. 'Just a bit grand for us, isn't it?'

'Are we going to dance on that?' Ben didn't sound very enthusiastic. Elaine looked at him quickly. He didn't seem to be as happy as she was. He kept complaining about the food and the crowds, and he now had a rather bad-tempered look on his face.

'Sure,' Shaz said, looking at him too. 'Anything wrong?'

'You are tired maybe?' Haruko said. 'You will be able to cope with the rehearsal and the performance?'

'Of course I'll be able to cope with it,' Ben replied. Even to Elaine it sounded rude, and she could tell from the way Haruko's eyebrows went up a little that it sounded rude to her too.

Shaz had jumped down the wide, shallow stairs and up onto the stage. She made a couple of slow, graceful turns across the floor.

'It's smaller than you're used to,' she called up to them. 'But I love the fact it's completely in the round. It really suits the piece we're presenting.'

Haruko stepped down more deliberately, and joined Shaz on the stage. Her face went calm and blank, and Elaine could see now the butō dancer that Shaz had shown them on a video before they came. The Japanese woman's face was so still that every slight change of expression registered. Elaine watched enviously. She wished she could move like that, be like that.

She was so glad she was here! There was so much she

could learn.

Next to her Ben shifted restlessly. Haruko noticed—she notices everything, Elaine thought—and came up the steps. 'Come,' she said, 'I'll take you to have a drink. At least you have seen the space you will be performing in. And then we will look at the rehearsal space. We are able to use one of the music studios.' She was being kind, but Elaine thought she seemed disappointed in them. 'We probably seem like spoiled kids to her,' she thought.

'Can I just try the stage?' she asked.

Haruko smiled broadly. 'Of course, of course. Please!'

Elaine joined Shaz on the stage, and slowly, for they were not warmed up, they went through one of the routines. Elaine couldn't believe she was going to be dancing in this space—there were an awful lot of chairs, which meant they'd be performing in front of an awful lot of people. The thought was terrifying and exhilarating.

When they rejoined Haruko and Ben, Ben whispered to her, 'Suck!'

'It's what we're here to do,' she said sharply. 'What's wrong with you?'

He didn't answer. He couldn't put it into words. Coming away to this strange country had brought all sorts of unusual feelings to the surface. He was homesick, he didn't like the food, he felt unsure of himself all the time, he hated being stared at, he wasn't sure he could face performing on that stage in front of all those people. And there was something going on in his mind which he didn't like. He kept having thoughts which he didn't recognise as his.

'Hey,' Elaine said, 'it'll be okay. It's going to be great.'

When he didn't respond she said, 'Let's go and have a drink, like Haruko said. And something to eat. They'll probably have fries here. It looks like that sort of a place.'

They went to a café on the atrium floor. It was called 'Enfants', which Haruko explained was French for children.

'I know that,' Ben said. 'We do study French in Australian schools, you know!' The name itself irritated him. He wasn't an enfant. He was fourteen, nearly grown up for heaven's sake! All the Japanese he met treated people his age as children, and the kids looked and acted like children too, far younger, it seemed, than people that age in Australia.

'Where do you come from?' Elaine asked Haruko, to make up for the raised eyebrows she had observed again.

'I grew up in the west of Japan, near Hiroshima,' Haruko said.

'Oh!' Elaine didn't quite know what to say next. Haruko was far too young to have been alive in the war, but perhaps her parents...

'I wish we had time to go there,' Shaz said, drinking her black coffee very quickly. 'I'd love to go back. It's the most amazing city,' she told Elaine.

'Isn't it, like, very sad?' Elaine said tentatively.

'It's tragic. I just howled my eyes out. The paper cranes on Sadako's monument—do you know there were bunches of them from schoolchildren in New Zealand and Australia? And the museum. Everyone should go there to see what war can do. But Hiroshima is wonderful too. It's got the wildest, strongest sense of life to it.' Shaz looked at Haruko. 'Almost as if the people there have been through the worst and survived, and so nothing can ever scare them again.'

Haruko smiled. 'Maybe,' she said. 'Or maybe that is because we are from the warm west—not cold like these northerners in Tokyo!'

'But you aren't scared of anything,' Elaine exclaimed without quite knowing why she said it.

'My dance is all about fear,' Haruko replied. 'I have to know fear to dance it.' She finished her coffee. 'But we are getting very serious. Now we will go and have fun. I will show you some interesting places near here. I think you will like. Many young people there.'

They looked quickly into the music studio where they would be rehearsing during the week. It was full of cute little kids playing violins, watched by their elegant and adoring mothers.

As they walked through the atrium to the escalators that led back to the street, Haruko pointed out the huge television monitor. 'This has all the programs on it. See, now is the information for the Youth Arts Festival. That little figure is the logo for it. He is cute, isn't he?'

Ben and Elaine stared at the screen. The logo was a cartoon character of a white dove. It had a fat white chest, partly covered by a blue jacket with an olive branch embroidered on it. It flapped its wings and waved to a group of cartoon children who were running into a cartoon Children's Castle, all smiling very happily.

'Bit corny, isn't it?' Ben muttered to Elaine. 'And it's not exactly the sort of dance we're doing, is it?'

He felt suddenly terribly angry. He hated the stupid white dove. The whole trip was obviously going to be a disaster. He glared at the screen. He felt power flow through him. The only way not to be afraid was to be angry. Anger released him momentarily from the paralysis of homesickness. He felt he could destroy all the hypocrisy and pretence and make people see things as they really were.

The dove squawked in outrage. The screen flashed dark purple and then went snowy. There was a small explosive sound and then the monitor blanked out. The lights in the atrium flickered. The escalators stopped, sending a group of children flying off the end.

Then everything started up again. The children were giggling. The dove returned. Haruko said calmly, 'For a moment I thought it might be an earthquake!' She stepped nimbly onto the down escalator.

'Earthquake?' Ben exclaimed. 'There's not likely to be one now, is there? While we're here?' His anger faded, and fear surfaced again.

'There've probably been a few already,' Shaz told him, as they left the Children's Castle and followed Haruko into the street. 'Tokyo has several small shocks every month.'

'How big do the shocks have to get before they're dangerous?' Ben looked around nervously. The broad street they were walking down and the narrow ones that led off it all looked equally vulnerable. What did you do in an earthquake? Hide under tables? Or in the bathroom like people did during Cyclone Tracy? Fear hovered over him all the time here. He'd never been homesick before and he had no idea what a disabling emotion it could be.

'How do people live with the threat of earthquakes?' Elaine asked. 'If it was me I'd be petrified all the time.'

'Typhoon mind,' Haruko said, smiling a little sardonically. 'They close their mind until it happens. Then when it's over they forget about it again.'

'Don't they have special buildings?'

'We're told everything is all right,' Haruko said. 'Very Japanese. We say it is all right, we say we know what's going to happen, and we believe we are forewarned, and so it will be all right. But the Kobe earthquake proved us wrong.'

'This is all so bizarre,' Ben muttered. 'I wish I could go home!'

From Tokyo Eki to Hamamatsucho, through Shibuya and Harajuko, Midori kept a close eye on the names of the stations, not daring to sit down in case she missed Shinjuku. When she finally found herself safely off the train and on the platform, she had no idea how to get out of the station. It was the most confusing place she'd ever been in. Miles and miles of tiled passageways led her where she didn't want to go and then refused to lead her out again. She asked several people to show her the right exit, but though they gave her careful directions, she never seemed to be able to follow them.

A miniature blue-and-yellow cleaning robot was trundling along the corridors, playing the same few bars of music from *Swan Lake* over and over as it brushed the side of the walls. Midori knew it was *Swan Lake* because one of the few things she remembered about her mother was going to the ballet with her just before she became ill. They had bought the CD afterwards and had played it at home while Midori pretended to be a ballerina. For a while she'd desperately wanted to take ballet lessons, but her mother had got so sick so suddenly and had died so quickly that the ballet lessons had never happened. Afterwards Midori had played *Swan Lake* whenever she felt like crying, and for a year or more it had always reduced her to tears. Then she decided she hated it for its sentimentality and slushiness, and she'd never played it since.

The third time she passed the robot Midori yelled at it in frustration: 'Stop playing that awful music and show me how to get out of here!'

Swan Lake ground to a discordant halt. The robot stopped dead in its tracks. Then, to Midori's astonishment, it obediently took off. She followed it as it threaded its way unerringly across the station, through the crowds and into the basement of a department store. It stopped at the foot of an escalator. Obviously it couldn't go up it.

Midori could see daylight ahead. She went up the escalator and at the top looked back. The robot gave an encouraging burst of music—*Swan Lake* played at triple speed—and then trundled away again. Midori felt rather lonely without it, but at the entrance to the department store she saw a sign that gave directions to several hotels, among them the Tokyo Hilton. She set out from the Nishiguchi down a long avenue that led towards the Shinjuku Central Park.

Meanwhile the robot went in search of an elevator. It had to wait for someone to operate the controls, and then it rolled in, got out at the ground floor and set off down the same avenue in pursuit of Midori.

Midori walked into the Hilton. It was huge and looked impressively expensive but she had stayed in hotels like this with her father many times and she was not fazed by it.

She decided not to ask for the Hayfords at reception, where somebody might later recall her face. She felt she had to be secretive and wary. Looking carefully around the lobby, she went to one of the pay phones and called the hotel's front desk from there, using the last yen on her phone card. In her American voice, not her Japanese one, she asked to speak to Dr Hayford. She'd been planning her story on the train.

When the Australian voice answered, she spoke, consciously making herself sound warm and friendly. 'Hello, I'm a friend of Midori Ito's.'

'Oh yes?' Rob answered, his voice immediately warm and

friendly too.

'Midori was hoping so much to meet your son, but she's had to go away. She asked me to phone you, maybe take Andrew out, do some sightseeing, that sort of thing?'

'That's very nice of you.' He sounded doubtful, but Midori wasn't going to be thwarted, having got this far.

'I'll come up right away,' she said firmly. 'I'm in the hotel lobby. You just give me your room number.'

Rob found himself telling her.

'Are you sure that was a good idea?' Rose watched the elevator doors close behind Andrew and the Japanese girl. She stepped back into the room and looked at Rob quizzically.

'There's nothing to worry about,' Rob assured her. 'Tokyo's the safest city in the world. Especially if you're with someone who speaks the language. Amazing girl. I could have sworn she was American on the phone. Their main problem would be getting lost, but that's not likely to happen. They're only going to Harajuko—just a couple of stops on the subway.'

Rose continued to look worried. She was remembering how the girl and Andrew had exchanged a very strange look when they set eyes on each other, almost as if they'd met before but they weren't going to let on about it.

Rob put his arms round her and kissed her. 'Come on, the girl's a godsend. You wanted us to be alone on this trip—well, now we are. We've got the whole day alone together and we're going to make the most of it. And Andrew will have a lot more fun with someone his own age.'

He hung the 'Do not disturb' sign on the door and pulled it shut. Then he took the phone off the hook.

Andrew took a quick look at the girl striding down the pavement next to him. He couldn't remember what her name was—had she said Keiko or Seiko? She looked vaguely familiar to him, but he couldn't think where he would have met anyone like her. She was scowling fiercely. In her blue jeans and plaid jacket she didn't look at all like the demure young ladies in kimono that covered the walls of the Japanese classroom at his school. Her long black hair streamed over her shoulders. He could imagine her riding into battle, wielding a sword, or hurling large men over her shoulder in the dōjō.

'So what happened to Professor Ito?' he asked, trotting a little to keep up with her.

The girl turned angrily towards him. 'Don't talk so loudly!'

'Why? What's up? What's going on?'

Their eyes met again and he felt as he'd felt in the hotel room: as if he were beginning to understand something, but he had no idea what. It was just that when he looked at this girl and their eyes met, it made him feel more intelligent, closer to understanding ... whatever it was.

'Where are we going?' He decided he would keep on asking questions until she answered them. He was pretty sure they were not just going sightseeing.

Her fierceness was now tempered with something else. For a moment she looked softer, almost helpless. 'I don't know,' she admitted. 'I've found you, but I don't know what to do next.'

'Who are you really?' Andrew said. 'You're not really Keiko or Seiko or whatever you said.'

She looked up and down the street as though searching for someone. Then she pulled Andrew into a small coffee shop. 'Let's sit down and talk. I need to explain things to you. And you must tell me what you know.'

They sat down at a tiny table at the back of the shop. The girl ordered drinks for them both, cola for Andrew and hot chocolate for herself. They didn't say much while they were waiting for the drinks. Andrew looked at the astonishing photos of dishes on the menu and tried to decipher the katakana. He had managed ice cream sundae, largely by guesswork, when the waitress put the drinks in front of them with a muttered 'Onegaishimasu.'

Then the girl leaned across the table and whispered to him, 'I am Midori Ito. Professor Ito is my father.'

Andrew stared at her. 'Why all the secrecy?'

'I'm not sure.' Midori frowned. She looked around the coffee shop. It seemed an ordinary place, with a tired but cheerful looking waitress, and an older woman on the till. There were a few other customers, mostly girls her own age or a little older, two men in suits, two women in kimono. No other foreigners.

She looked back at Andrew. He stood out too much. His hair was too blond. Even in the coffee shop people kept sneaking surreptitious glances at him, and at one table the girls had started talking in English to attract his attention.

'Good morning? How are you?' they were saying to each other and then collapsing into fits of giggles.

Andrew took a sip of his cola. It tasted almost like Coke, but not quite. He frowned as he thought about it, letting the cold, sweet liquid slip down his throat. It was foreign. Like everything else. He looked through the window at the street outside. It was full of people. He'd never seen so many all at once. And they all looked so alike. He wished the girls in the corner would stop staring at him. What did they think he was, some sort of freak? He felt a kind of anger sweep through him.

The cash register pinged and opened its drawer. The woman on the desk made a quiet exclamation. It sounded like 'Shimatta.'

On the snowy hillside the white-clad figure moved forward silently. He stopped. He saw tracks in the snow. Small feet, like a woman's. So, she was still ahead of him...

Further up the slope he saw a flash of red, a white-tipped brush.

The only tracks in the snow now were of fox feet.

'Did you do that?' Midori whispered. Andrew didn't know what he had done, but something had happened, something like what had happened to the automatic drinks machine at the airport. He was saved from having to answer by a sudden disturbance outside the window. People were standing around and pointing. A woman with a little girl jumped out of the way, pulling the child with her.

Midori was about to say something else, but she stopped with her mouth open.

The crowd cleared outside the window. A small blue-and-yellow robotic cleaner stood on the footpath. Even through the glass Andrew could hear that it was playing some fast and chirpy music.

'I don't believe it!' Midori said. 'That thing's followed me from Shinjuku station.'

She got to her feet and gestured to Andrew. 'Come on,' she said. 'I don't like this. We'd better try and get away from it.'

The robot followed them back to Shinjuku. It became quite agitated when they escaped down the escalator.

Andrew glanced back and saw it for a moment at the top of the stairs. The music went faster than ever. Then the robot reversed purposefully and disappeared.

'Where are we going?' he panted as Midori raced him off the escalator and down what seemed like interminable passages.

'I don't know!' she confessed. 'We've got to talk but I'm afraid of giving things away.'

'Who to?' he demanded. People swept past them on their way to trains, but there was no one around who seemed to be watching them or listening to them.

'I don't know,' she said again. 'Perhaps we'd better act like tourists.' There was a short pause. She seemed to be concentrating. Then her face cleared. 'We'll do what I told your father we were going to do. We'll go to Harajuko.'

Andrew was sure he'd never heard the name before. Had Rose mentioned it to him? He didn't think so. But as soon as Midori said 'Harajuko' he knew that was where they had to go.

They made a few false turns, and Midori had to ask for directions a couple of times, but eventually they found their way back to the Yamanote loop. Andrew was impressed. He hated to admit it, but he was overawed by Tokyo. It was immeasurably huger than anywhere he'd ever been, and even though some of the names and signs were in English, mostly he was totally confused by the directions, and the kanji everywhere. With some perseverance, he found he could decipher the words in hiragana—*kudasai* seemed to follow a lot of the instructions—but without Midori he would have been completely lost.

The train when it arrived was fairly crowded but not packed.

'Lucky it's Sunday,' Midori said, as they found seats side by side. 'It would be very much more crowded during the week.'

Andrew looked around the carriage. Above the seats there were advertisements he couldn't read, though he recognised some of the brand names, and signs in kanji near the doors that he assumed meant 'non-smoking', 'second class' and so on. Most people took no notice of him—foreigners were quite common on the Yamanote line—but an old man in a seat opposite was staring at him with a look of outrage.

Andrew nudged Midori. 'Am I doing something wrong? Why's that old guy staring at me?'

Midori studied the old man and then patted Andrew reassuringly on the arm. 'Take no notice. If he was following us he wouldn't be so obvious. He probably thinks you're American. Some people still remember the war. They don't like foreigners.'

'I'm a foreigner here,' Andrew said to himself. It was the

first time it had dawned on him. It shook his confidence a little.

Everyone around him looked the same—only he looked different. It was a most peculiar feeling. He looked different and he was different—inside especially. He couldn't read the signs around him, he couldn't understand the language. He was completely dependent on the girl next to him.

He sneaked a quick glance at her, and realised with a sudden shock that he had no idea who she really was. Perhaps she wasn't even Professor Ito's daughter. Perhaps she was someone else, sent to kidnap him. The professor had sounded so strange on the phone. Would he really have let his daughter come to Tokyo on her own?

As if she could read his thoughts, Midori looked at him and grinned. Her fierce face was immediately transformed. 'Don't worry,' she said quietly. 'We'll be okay. But I think we have to find the others.'

'The others?'

'The ones who are still missing.'

Andrew felt the same way he'd felt when she'd decided to go to Harajuko, as if he both knew and didn't know what she was talking about. 'I've got to stay with you,' he said candidly. 'Because I don't know where I am and I'd never work out the trains without you. But you could be anyone. How do I even know you're Professor Ito's daughter?'

Midori said, 'You have to trust me.' After a short pause she went on, 'Do you remember how you had to replace the gun in the first game?'

'In Space Demons?'

'Yes. You didn't know what would happen. You had to trust.'

'I know,' Andrew said with feeling. 'And I thought the game was tricking me all the time. It was only Elaine ...'

'Elaine!' Midori exclaimed.

'What about her?'

'She's one of the others!'

'Do you know what's going on?' Andrew knew Midori was right. Elaine was one of the others they had to find, to reunite, to make…he had no idea what. But he had all these strange ideas floating through his head, half thoughts, half dreams: some of them his, some quite foreign to him. He was being led somewhere, in the same way as he had already been led to Tokyo, and Midori had been led to meet up with him. A draught of chill air swept into the train and he shivered.

'Not exactly,' Midori said. 'But I'm starting to get an idea. Come on, this is Harajuko. This is where we get off.'

It seemed that most of the other passengers on the train were going there too. Andrew and Midori followed a stream of well-dressed young people up the stairs and into the street. Across the road from the station entrance was a maze of small streets and shops, some of them only a few metres across, stocked with trendy clothes and accessories. Groups of teenagers pushed patiently through the crowds, their basic good manners unaltered by their outrageous hairstyles and clothes. Andrew saw girls who would have been Gothics in Australia. They wore black gear, but their hair was dyed red or blonde. He thought they looked weird but fantastic. And it was nice to see a few other people with fair hair.

'You should dye your hair black,' Midori commented, as though she had been reading his thoughts again. 'You wouldn't stand out so much. If anyone's watching us, you'd be instantly recognisable.'

'Who'd be watching us?' Andrew said, as he followed her up the stairs of the overhead crossing. 'And I've been meaning to ask you, how come you speak such great English?'

Midori smiled. 'My father spent two years working in

America. I went to elementary school there. I was only nine—you learn foreign languages quickly at that age.'

'Do most Japanese people speak such good English?' Andrew was feeling rather ashamed of his extremely basic Japanese.

'Most people my age would love to be able to speak English. It's very chic at the moment. Older people think everyone ought to learn Japanese, but at the same time they are quite suspicious of foreigners who speak Japanese too well! At least, that's what I've heard Dad say.'

Andrew was silent for a moment. He was determined to study harder when the school year started again. He would learn more Japanese. He would get to speak it...

Midori broke into his thoughts. 'Andoru-san wa nihongo ga dekimasuka?'

Andrew caught the *nihongo,* guessed what she was asking and shook his head. 'Iie.'

'Sukoshi?'

He shook his head again. 'Hardly anything really.'

'Come on, say something.' He realised she was teasing him. He liked it. When she was serious she looked as fierce as a warrior, and when she smiled she was really pretty. The contrast fascinated him.

'Okay. Andrew Hayford desu. Hajimemashite.'

'Dōzo yoroshiku,' she answered gravely. He racked his brains to think of something else and finally came up with 'Doko ni ikimasuka?'

'Hey, that's very good,' she said. 'But I think I'd better tell you in English, because I don't think you'll understand much. How long have you been learning?'

'Just this year.' Words were coming to him thick and fast now. He looked at the trees and translated them into *ki,* the park they were approaching was *kōen*—but he didn't know the words in any language for what he saw ahead of him on the street.

A blare of fifties rock music was echoing through the park from nineties ghetto blasters placed on the bitumen. Jiving to the music was a whole group of Elvis Presley lookalikes— black jeans, shoestring ties, blue suede shoes. Further down were other groups, each in their own particular uniform, with rival music competing for ear space.

'Wow!' Andrew said. 'This is totally crazy!'

Behind the Elvis Presleys was another group. Most of them had shaved heads, some wore robes like monks and some wore traditional Japanese dress. One or two even had the old-fashioned samurai hairstyle that Andrew knew from movies. They formed a strange contrast, almost like a reproach, to the noisy, jiving rock star impersonators. Above their heads flew flags and banners with an emblem of a wide-open eye with a blue teardrop in the place of the pupil.

'Who are they?' Andrew asked.

'They're a new sect. Very traditional. Pure Mind, they're called.' Midori didn't say anything else but Andrew noticed that she scanned the faces of the men in the group, and then turned her head away quickly as though she were afraid of being recognised.

There was a statue in the middle of the footpath. Andrew was about to go round it when it moved. It wasn't a statue at all but a person, naked except for a loincloth, and painted grey all over. The statue moved with slight, infinitesimal gestures, oblivious to the sea of people around it. Across its stone-like face flickered an expression of pain.

Andrew lingered to watch as the orderly crowds swept past, some stopping to watch the living statue too, others moving on with a smile. On the edge of the crowd a small figure caught his eye. It was a woman, a Westerner. Because she didn't move on he felt she was connected with the statue. She had streaky, straw-coloured hair and a pale face. Thin and bony, she was wearing black baggy trousers and a thick quilted plaid shirt of the sort popular with many Japanese teenage boys. The crowds cleared around her momentarily, and he saw a hat at her feet. She was guarding the statue's money. She looked across the space between them and grinned at Andrew.

She reminded him of Elaine Taylor. Something about the shape of her face and the way she stood was just like Elaine, and so was the fearless, open smile. Then the crowds swirled again between them and he couldn't see her any more.

He was thinking about Elaine—he and Midori had been talking about her on the train, and now he had seen someone who had reminded him of her. So when he saw her across the road, it took him a few seconds to do a double-take. This was Japan for heaven's sake, the middle of Tokyo. He had to be wrong. Why on earth would Elaine Taylor be here? She was in Adelaide. It was just one of the Japanese Gothic girls who looked like her from the back or from the side—same shape, same red hair ...

But it wasn't a Japanese girl. It was Elaine, because she had seen him, and she was waving to him. She was looking mildly astonished, but not as amazed as he was.

'Midori.' Andrew caught her arm and turned her towards him. 'The most extraordinary thing ... You know the girl we were talking about before, Elaine Taylor? You said she was one of the others.'

Midori nodded, her dark eyes fixed and intent.

'She's over there,' Andrew said. 'On the other side of the road. And Ben's there with her!' His amazement was now complete.

'Don't look so surprised,' Midori said. 'That's why we had to come here. Don't you understand?'

'Understand what?' Andrew said. 'I don't think I understand anything.'

He was feeling completely disoriented, as though the whole world had just tipped over and everything had slid out of place.

'We're being drawn together,' Midori said. 'We're finding each other. Or something is finding us.'

The Japanese walking past smiled indulgently at the three excited Australians who had just met on the footpath. Impossible though it might seem, here they were all together in central Tokyo. They couldn't stop exclaiming about it.

Then Shaz Christie appeared out of the crowd with Haruko.

Andrew noticed how much Midori changed when she was speaking Japanese to the other woman. She became almost a different person, graver and more submissive. She bowed formally to Haruko and shook hands with Shaz Christie, who exclaimed over her English.

Midori briefly repeated the story of her American experiences, but she made no mention of her father.

'Haruko-san is a dancer and the director of the Youth Arts Festival we've been invited to be part of,' Shaz explained. 'So she's showing us some of the sights of Tokyo.' She waved one lanky arm around her head. Her silver bangles clashed and shone in the winter sun. 'I'd heard about this place. It's fabulous.'

No one spoke. The four teenagers looked at each other, and looked away again. They were no longer laughing and exclaiming. Their eyes changed and went hard.

'Let's walk on a little,' Haruko suggested, thinking that perhaps they wanted the adults out of the way.

The two women went on ahead. They made a strange couple. Shaz was so much taller than her friend that she had to bend over to hear what Haruko was saying. But in Harajuko to be strange is to fit in, so the glances they attracted were all admiring.

The others followed them at a distance. 'I can't believe you're here too,' Andrew kept saying to Elaine and Ben. 'It's uncanny.'

'We nearly died when Mars told us you were already in Japan,' Elaine said.

'Mars! He should be here too! What's he up to?'

'Probably breaking into someone's house to get on to the Net,' Ben said. 'Darren wouldn't let him near our computer any more after he upset it.'

'What did he do to it?'

'It went into overdrive and seized up.'

'Weird!'

'Everything's a bit weird,' Ben said, shivering. 'Isn't this just the weirdest place you've ever been to?'

The fact that they were all standing there together was enough to blow anyone's mind.

'And who are you?' Ben said to Midori. 'Midori what? I've got the feeling I know you from somewhere.'

'Can I tell them?' Andrew asked her. Midori nodded, pulling him off the path and into the trees. Ben and Elaine followed.

Midori looked round anxiously. 'I'm afraid of being noticed,' she said quietly.

'Noticed?' Ben said. 'There are about five million people out there. How can you not be noticed?'

'I mean by someone who knows me, or who knows my father. To be here with you three is very...' For the first time she stumbled for the right word. 'Conspicuous,' she went on. 'You all stand out so much. People will look. If they know about you they'll know what to look for.'

'I'm completely lost!' Ben said. 'Who could be looking for us?'

'The same people who are looking for my father.'

'So who is your father?'

Elaine had said nothing so far. She had been listening, both to Midori and to the voice echoing faintly inside her head. Now she spoke for the first time. 'You're Professor Ito's daughter, aren't you?'

Midori nodded. She and Elaine looked at each other, the black eyes meeting the grey ones. They both recalled shared visions, fears, hopes. Elaine went on, 'And this is all to do with the games your father sent Andrew.'

'Hey,' Ben said. 'Mario sent away for the next game. Did he ever get it?'

'There are no more games,' Midori said. 'My father was working on a new one when people started putting pressure on him to market the first two. He felt something was going wrong somewhere. He wasn't happy about some of the ways the games developed when they were played by other people. The programs seemed to be writing themselves, going further than he had ever intended.'

'You've played them too, haven't you?' Elaine said.

'Yes, but different things happened when I played. It's as though the program reacts with the personality of the player.'

'Your dad made a big mistake sending the games to Andrew,' Ben remarked. 'No wonder they're having strange developments!'

'It's not something to joke about,' Midori said, turning her fierce gaze on him. 'My father is in real danger. He's left our home in Osaka and is trying to hide.'

'He didn't even come to meet us,' Andrew put in. 'And he phoned me and sounded really stressed on the phone.'

'The people my father used to work for would stop at nothing to get their hands on the games,' Midori said. 'And on all of us too.'

'Why us?' Ben said. 'What have we got to do with it?'

'We're the ones who've played the games,' Midori said. 'We modified and changed the program. And now the program is trying to play us.'

They stared at her in disbelief.

'Don't you feel it?' she cried. 'Why else would we all be here together? How did I know I had to get Andrew from the Hilton and then come to Harajuko? How come you two just happened to turn up here? Something's drawing us together! We played the earlier games and now we are essential for the next game. Anyone who wants to control it is going to have to control it through us.'

Elaine scowled at her. It was a horrible idea and she didn't want it to be true. Being invited to Tokyo with Shaz Christie had been the best thing that had ever happened to her. She wanted it to be because she was a gifted dancer, not because some strange power had intruded into her life and was using her.

'I think we should catch up with Shaz,' she said, turning to walk back onto the road. 'She'll be wondering where on earth we are.'

'We have to stay together,' Midori said urgently.

'You're mad,' Ben said and followed Elaine. Down the street they could see Shaz's tall, thin shape. They glimpsed the pale splash of her face as she turned to scan the road behind her. She was looking for them.

Elaine wanted more than anything to get back to Shaz but she found it hard to leave Midori and Andrew. It felt as if she really were being bound to them by some supernatural power. Each step away made her head pound. But Ben took her by the arm and pulled her down the street. He still looked pale and unhappy, as he had since they had been in Japan, but if his head was aching too he didn't mention it.

Before Midori and Andrew could catch up with them,

two men approached Elaine and Ben. One was a Japanese businessman in a suit, the other a Westerner, more casually dressed.

'Hey, kid,' the second man addressed Ben, in an accent halfway between Australian and American. 'Can I ask a favour of you?'

Disarmed by the Australian tones, Ben nodded.

'Can you take a photo of me and my friend here?' The man held out an expensive automatic camera. 'Just point and click.'

'Sure,' Ben said. The two men stood stiffly in front of him, the Elvis Presleys visible in the background. Ben lined up the shot carefully and pressed the button.

'Thanks, mate.' The man who sounded Australian took back the camera and without asking took a quick snap of the two of them, Ben in the foreground and Elaine behind him. 'Just a souvenir, okay!' He felt in his pocket and took out a banknote—it looked like 5000 yen. 'Here, get yourself a Coke on me.'

Ben took the note with a muttered word of thanks and put it in his pocket. The two men waved and walked off.

Midori ran up to them and grabbed Ben's arm. Her face had gone almost completely white. 'I think I recognised that man, the Japanese one. I'm sure it's one of the bosses from E3, the managing director. I think his name is Mr Kinoshita.' Her voice broke off. She swallowed and went on quietly, 'The other one could have been Mr Miller! It must have been him!'

Ben shook his arm free from her hold.

Andrew demanded, 'Who's Miller?'

'He's one of the people looking for Dad!' Midori said angrily to Ben. 'What did they say to you?'

'Just asked me to take their photo,' Ben replied. 'They were harmless. Just tourists like us.'

'He took your photo too, didn't he?'

'Hey,' Ben replied. 'He was Australian. He was just being

nice. Why on earth should it be this Miller, or whatever his name is? There must be thousands of Australians in Tokyo. This is a tourist spot—it's Sunday, the sun's shining. This is where all the tourists come.'

'Did he give you anything?' Midori asked.

'No,' Ben replied, staring her down. He felt a twinge of warning somewhere at the back of his mind but he ignored it. Midori was really annoying him with her air of knowing more than anyone else. Like Elaine, he didn't want to believe that what she said was true. He didn't really want to be in Tokyo at all, but if he had to be there he wanted it to be through his own choice, not because of some sinister force. And if he had to be there, it would help to have a little more cash. Midori, with her expensive clothes and American education, would never understand that.

Ben was changing, Elaine thought, as she watched him. He must have been changing all year and she hadn't noticed, but coming away to a foreign country had made it more obvious to her. For a start he had suddenly begun to grow—he was taller than she was now—and he had become much more independent and almost bossy. She recalled how he had stood up to his older brother, Darren, at the end of the Skymaze game, and had declared then that he was never going to let anyone push him around again. Midori was right: the games had affected their characters. She wondered what other changes were already taking place. Thinking about it made her feel lonely and afraid.

Ben gave Midori a challenging stare.

Midori looked away, scowling, then seemed to freeze as she glanced back into the crowds on the roadway.

Andrew followed her gaze. The tall Australian who had taken the photo was in intense conversation with the Japanese man. They looked as if they were trying to observe the group of young people without actually looking at them. Or was he imagining it? Since he had been in Tokyo he seemed to be imagining all sorts of things. Was it just that he was in a foreign country, or was there really something going on inside his head which was beginning to get out of control?

Elaine tugged on Ben's arm. 'We must catch up with Shaz,' she said again anxiously.

'Sure,' he said. 'Come on, Andrew, come with us. We can tell you where we're staying—and you can come and see the show.'

The living statue had moved down the street a little and was now just opposite the shrubs where they had been talking. Elaine stopped dead, and stared at the small woman who was still standing by the hat on the ground.

'Do you know her?' Andrew said. 'It's funny, but I saw her earlier and she reminded me of you.'

Elaine shook herself. She didn't reply, just hurried past the woman with her head turned away. Andrew looked back. The woman was staring after them. Like Elaine, she looked as if she'd seen a ghost.

Shaz and Haruko had gone further ahead than they'd re-alised, but Elaine could see them far in the distance, Shaz standing out because she was taller than almost anyone else in the crowd. They had stopped by a group of fifties rockers in tight black jeans and black leather jackets. 'Rock Around the Clock' blared from six synchronised tape decks. Shaz gave her bag to Haruko and began to dance.

Midori was talking urgently to Andrew. He frowned as he listened, then nodded and quickened his steps to catch up with Elaine and Ben.

'Those men are still following us,' he said quietly in Elaine's ear. Ben had stopped to look at a street vendor's display of jewellery. The salesman wasn't Japanese, but looked as if he might be from Iran, or some other Middle Eastern country. Rose had told Andrew about Japan's foreign workers, and how lonely many of them were, living without their families in a country not noted for its ready acceptance of foreigners.

'They can't do anything to us if we're with Shaz and Haruko,' Elaine answered. 'Let's just catch up with them and stay with them. They can come back to your hotel with you if you're worried.'

'Elaine,' he said seriously, 'I don't think it's a question of just going back and everything will be all right. Something's started up, and everything's changing. Can't you feel it?'

'Yes,' she replied, her face pale with concentration. 'I can feel it. Inside my head. Things are changing. It's as if I can do anything, make dreams come true. But other people want that power. They want to get us, control us. Maybe we shouldn't be together. Maybe we should try to fight what's happening. Put a stop to it now.'

Midori said, 'I'm not happy here. I think we should go.'

'Hang on,' Ben said. 'I want to get something for my mother.'

'You can do that later! Let's get out of here.' Andrew pulled at his arm.

Ben ignored him. 'Do you like this one or this one best?' he said to Elaine, holding up two bead necklaces, one blue, one purple.

'Either,' she replied shortly. 'It doesn't matter.' She had caught a sense of urgency from Midori, and she wanted to get back to Shaz and Haruko.

'You American?' the street seller asked.

'No way!' Ben replied. 'We're Australians.'

'Australian!' The man's dark face broke into a broad smile. 'Sydney?'

'No, Adelaide actually.'

'Ben,' Andrew warned him. 'This guy doesn't want to know your life history.'

'My cousin is in Sydney,' the man said.

'Wow! How about that! Whereabouts?'

'Marrittville?'

'Marrickville,' Andrew said shortly.

'Your English is pretty good,' Ben said, refusing to be hurried. 'Do you speak Japanese too?'

'Japanese, English, Arabic,' he replied. 'And a little German.'

'Wow!' Ben said again. 'Can't you get a better job?'

The man gave him a strange look full of weariness and cynicism. 'I would like to live in Australia,' he said. 'But very hard to get visa.'

'Isn't it hard here?'

The man gave him the same look. 'Why do you think I sell on the street?' His mood changed. 'Come on,' he said. 'I make you good price for this one. Good price for the Australian mother. She'll like it, I think. Eight hundred yen.'

Ben fumbled in his pocket for the unfamiliar money. He took out the 5000-yen note the Australian had given him. The Iranian looked at it and gave it back. 'Sorry, no change,' he said. 'You got small money?'

Ben held out some coins on the palm of his hand. The man picked out a 500-yen coin and three 100s. 'Okay,' he said, putting the necklace in a small brown envelope. 'Have good holiday. Good luck!'

Midori was scowling more than ever. 'Come on,' she said angrily to Ben. 'Don't waste any more time.'

Ben was about to retort, 'What's the rush?' and deliberately examine everything really slowly just because he hated people trying to order him around, and he was finding this girl insufferable with her perfect English and her bossy manner, but he suddenly realised that people were pushing against him in a way that had nothing to do with the crowds on the street. A group of people in robes and traditional dress, looking quite expressionless and harmless, had surrounded them and as if by accident were herding them away from Shaz and Haruko, in the opposite direction to the one they wanted to go.

'Hey!' Ben said sharply to the person nearest him. 'Watch who you're pushing!'

'Sumimasen,' the man muttered. 'Shitsurei shimasu.' But he kept pushing just the same.

Midori said something very rapid and angry in Japanese, but it made no difference to the group. They simply continued their silent, inexorable movement, pushing the young people back down the street.

'Run,' the others heard Midori say. She didn't say anything aloud but they felt something deep inside their minds come awake, fuse and take over. They moved as one creature with many different parts but one will. Each of them made a sudden, elusive movement, like a choreographed step in a dance. They slipped through the wall of Pure Mind members, and ran together down the street.

You are happy. You are growing. You can feel your mind expanding. Its parts are being drawn together. Your power is increasing. You see with many eyes. You think with many cells. You are faster than any of those who try to impede you. You laugh at them as you slip away from them.

You see a brilliant, flashing world, pulsing with colour. It's almost overpowering, but though it overwhelms you now, you will learn all about it. Now that your mind is growing, it will not be long before you have control over this wonderful world of communication, this mass of brain cells which are all going to be yours. You extend your power into it and laugh again. You begin to play, to create…

At the entrance to Harajuko station they were slowed by the crowd. Behind them they could see the band of sect members pressing after them, moving slowly but unstoppably like a monster in a nightmare. Midori was trying to arrange tickets for all of them. The queues were huge.

'This is crazy,' Elaine said. 'What about Shaz? We must tell her where we're going.'

But then she caught sight of the pale faces and shaved heads of their pursuers, and she joined Midori in the frantic search for change for the ticket machines.

'Where are we going anyway?' she said.

'I don't know,' Midori exclaimed. 'The only place I can think of is Itako. If anyone can explain what's happening and will know what to do it's my father—but I'm afraid of giving away his hiding place to his enemies.'

The last of the tickets fell from the machine. Midori grabbed it. She gave a ticket to each of them.

But as they pushed through the automatic gates their pursuers were right after them. It seemed as if they would prevent them from getting on the train. Again they felt themselves surrounded. The sinister group seemed to expand in size and increase in number. The pressure against them grew. They were being crushed, absorbed, devoured.

'Help!' Elaine screamed.

And suddenly help came from a completely unexpected source. There was a blare of music, and the robot cleaner, brushes whirring, swept up from behind and knocked the group aside.

Relentlessly it cruised up and down the forecourt, clearing more people aside with every turn. *Swan Lake* rang through the air.

Suddenly Elaine saw that the way ahead was clear. The others realised it at the same time. They ran for the stairs. A train was just stopping at the station. The doors opened and they piled on. Behind them they could see the mass of people trying to get past the robot. Then robot and shaved heads were gone as the train pulled away.

The three Australians and the Japanese girl looked at each other in relief and amazement.

'Would someone please explain to me what's going on?' Ben said.

Once back at Tokyo station Midori managed to find the way to the Itako line. It was late and growing colder, and already homeless people were moving into the subway passages to stake a claim to the warmest spots. Elaine looked at them in concern. They seemed incongruous in such a wealthy metropolis.

'Come on,' Midori urged her.

'Who are those people?'

'I don't know. Probably Koreans.'

'Doesn't anyone do anything to help them?' Ben asked. He was still disturbed by his conversation with the Iranian. He had a sense of the terrible injustice of life. He wished he could do something about it. How could people play at being American rock stars in Harajuko when there was so much wrong with their world? And why didn't religious groups help more people? Why didn't Professor Ito spend his time on useful inventions rather than these dumb games, come to that? He followed the others morosely onto the platform.

A rapid express was leaving in half an hour. They spent the time sampling the automatic vending machines, but Midori wouldn't let Andrew see if he could get the machine to work by staring at it again. There were too many JR officials watching them, and she felt they were already too conspicuous.

At first the train was too crowded for them to sit together, but after the stop at Narita, the city famous for its temples and shrines as well as its international airport, they found seats opposite each other and they could talk.

Looking back at the golden pagoda roof of the temple disappearing through the pine trees as the train started to speed up, Andrew could hardly believe it was only two days since he had arrived at the airport. And how different Narita looked from the train, compared with what he'd seen at the airport terminus. Now the train wound its way through rice paddies, bare apart from brownish winter stalks, cut into a chequerboard by raised banks. Small, densely wooded hills enclosed the cultivated land, and in the shelter of the hills were old-style farmhouses with curved tiled roofs. Apart from the television aerials, they looked as if they hadn't changed since they were built. The late afternoon light made the scene look diffuse and grainy, like an old film. Andrew half-expected to see samurai appear through the gap in the hills, and then gasped when he did see a man in traditional clothes, kimono, hanten and geta, walking purposefully towards his house. It was as though the centuries had rolled away.

When the train passed through villages and towns, the houses along the track were smaller, almost miniature. Andrew noticed the poles used for washing lines, quilts hung out to air on windowsills, bonsai trees, and once a tiny tractor in a lane. The streets in the towns were very narrow—they must have been built long before cars were invented—but that didn't stop motorists trying to drive down them.

At every station Midori went to the doors and checked the platform, but apart from the stares drawn by the Australians' fair hair and light eyes, no one seemed to be watching them.

Nevertheless, Elaine was in a panic. 'We must phone Shaz,' she said, sounding almost tearful. 'She'll be so worried about us. And we're supposed to start rehearsing tomorrow. What are she and Haruko going to think?'

'You have her phone number?' Midori said. 'We'll phone when we get to my grandmother's. My father will know what to do.'

'He will, won't he?' Ben's voice had a sneering tone to it.

Midori looked at him. 'What do you mean by that?'

He stared back at her without blinking. 'Just that if anyone wants us all together, it would be your father, wouldn't it? Do you know what we used to call him? The creepy professor. Do you know what creepy means?'

'Yes, I know what it means. But you're wrong.' Midori had flushed and her scowl was fiercer than ever. 'My father would never do anything to hurt anyone deliberately.'

'So how do you explain the weird games? And how come he sent them to us to play? Why didn't he try them out on you?' Ben was sounding increasingly hostile.

'Hey,' Andrew said, wanting to defend Midori. 'They weren't that bad.'

But Midori was perfectly capable of defending herself. 'I did play them. I played them both. Space Demons and Sky-maze. But I think they were different for me.' She looked at Andrew. 'I think they were more violent for you, weren't they? That was one of the things my father wanted to investigate—how violent the games would become and how much the personality of the player increased that violence. Toshi and I—' She paused, smiled to herself and shrugged. 'It's hard to explain.'

'Who's Toshi for a start?' Ben demanded.

'He's my father's assistant. He's worked with him since he graduated. He's brilliant.'

Ben looked doubtful. 'Suppose it's him who's trailing us?'

'No, I'm sure Toshi would never work for anyone but my father.' But Midori couldn't help remembering her conviction that Toshi was on his way to find her.

'So what happened when you and this Toshi played?' Andrew said. He remembered the game of Space Demons with a mixture of excitement and dread. He could hear the sinister voice of the program in his mind. It was hard to believe that the person who had written the program wasn't sinister as well. 'Did you get to the "respond to hate" bit?'

'It was different for us,' Midori said, evasively.

'How?' Ben challenged her.

'Did you actually get in the game and play from the inside?' Andrew asked.

'Yes, but not through hate.'

'So how?'

Midori's face went still. 'Through a kind of inner silence,' she said. 'It's very hard to explain. It's something you feel, something your inner self does. Toshi knows about it because he's always done jūdō and other martial arts. Well, I have too, of course.'

'Have you?' Andrew put in with interest.

Midori smiled. 'Actually I wanted to do ballet, or Spanish dancing. But Dad wanted me to do kendō—and anyway it was too hard to organise dance lessons. Kendō and jūdō are both taught at school. I don't mind. I quite like that sort of thing. It makes you strong. Not only physically, but inside.'

'Dance does the same thing,' Ben said, not wanting to be outfaced in any way. 'And gymnastics.'

'It could be different,' Elaine said slowly. 'It's like what Shaz was saying about dance—how we can learn so much from Japanese dance because it's full of meaning. It's not just movement, however beautiful.'

'We are all interested in similar things,' Midori said. 'But with a different approach maybe.'

'Andrew isn't,' Ben said. 'He never does anything more physical than move a mouse around.'

'I've got a very athletic mind,' Andrew said. 'Keyboard karate! Tell you what, though, the stuff I'd really like to know about is all that ninja stuff. That is so cool!'

'My father is concerned about young people,' Midori went on, ignoring Andrew for the time being.

Ben gave her a look of disbelief. She stared back challengingly at him and then plunged on, speaking very quickly. 'My cousin killed himself a few years ago. He was at a school in Tokyo and he was being very badly bullied. No one knew. The family were devastated. My father felt it terribly—it was his sister's only son and he was only thirteen. My father said that when he looked into the future he was very afraid for me, his own child, and for all other children. What hope is there for us in the world if we can't help each other and co-operate? When there are so many more people every decade and resources are running out, we must use everything we have with wisdom or we will all die out.'

'So we had to learn to give up the gun,' Elaine said, remembering Space Demons.

'That was the way the game led you,' Midori said. 'For Toshi and me it was slightly different. We had no gun. We faced the demons empty-handed and defeated them with techniques from martial arts. But in the end, to make them disappear altogether, we had to learn to embrace them.' She couldn't help shuddering. 'It was rather disgusting!'

'Guns aren't really an issue here?' Andrew said.

'Almost certainly not as much as in some Western countries. And of course, since the Second World War Japan hasn't been involved in the nuclear arms race, though arms deals go on, and my father would love to see them stopped.'

'Why did he pick us?' Andrew said. 'Or rather, me?'

'Partly circumstance,' Midori admitted with a smile. 'He had met your father several times when he was still working on computer diagnosis for hospitals. He was interested in Australia—it's Western but not American, it's part of Asia, it's got a lot of different races living together. It has many similarities to Japanese society and much that is almost the complete opposite. And it probably illustrates what much of the world will be like in the next century. My father believes that people are giving up on traditional morality. Everyone thinks that sooner or later technology and genetic engineering will make them better people, so why bother trying to be good? So we are at the end of an era, on the threshold of another, and it's through these computer games that young people can learn, and be changed.'

'So we were like an experiment for him?' Ben said accusingly.

'Sort of,' Midori agreed. 'Your father kept saying what a computer whiz you were,' she told Andrew. 'He even asked my father if he had any special games he could take back for you.'

'Rather a strong temptation, I'd imagine,' Andrew said. 'I didn't mind!'

'He shouldn't have done it, I suppose,' Elaine said quietly.

'But using one or two people could help so many,' Midori replied.

'I don't see how,' Ben objected. 'Why didn't he try and do something useful? Like something for those homeless people we keep seeing?'

Midori said seriously, 'People are being changed by technology. It's speeding up evolution. It's changing us, the way we think, the things we can do, the way we interact with the world and with each other. My father just wants that change to be good for people, and he thinks he's found a way to do it.'

'Through the games?' Elaine said.

'Yes, through the games.'

Andrew whistled. 'No wonder everyone's after him. The games must be worth a fortune.'

'It's not only the money they're worth,' Midori replied. 'It's the power they give people.' She leaned forward and said to Andrew, 'Remember the cash register? And the robot?'

He nodded. 'And the drinks machine at the airport.'

'There's something we can do,' Midori said. 'I'm not sure yet how to control it. But something happens inside our brains and it has an electronic reaction. It messes up computers, makes them behave in unpredictable ways—'

'Makes them do what we want,' Ben interrupted.

'And makes people do what we want,' Elaine added. 'How else did we all get here?' She stopped for a moment, a look of amazement crossing her face. 'No, that's too much,' she said. 'That can't be right!'

'What did you just think?' Midori said quickly.

'It's too stupid,' Elaine replied. 'It's just a fantasy.' Her eyes were bright with excitement, or sadness.

'What?' Andrew said.

'Makes dreams come true,' Elaine said diffidently.

Ben laughed, a sudden unpleasant noise.

Elaine said, 'I knew you'd think it was stupid. Forget it.'

'Why did you say that, Elaine?' Midori asked her. When Elaine didn't reply she said, 'You must tell us. We've all got to tell each other everything. We have to be completely truthful with each other.'

'I think I might have seen my mother at Harajuko,' Elaine replied.

Elaine's mother had left her and her father suddenly when Elaine was ten. One day she was there, just the same as usual: quick-tempered, unpredictable, funny, bossy; the next she was gone. Elaine's father never talked about her much, except one time when he had lost control and the story had all poured out. Elaine had been born when her mother was only seventeen. She'd been born prematurely and had spent weeks in hospital. When she came home, a difficult colicky baby who cried a lot, her mother had left her mostly in the care of her father. And then one day the woman who had never really wanted to be either a mother or a wife had gone, leaving neither explanation nor address.

Elaine used to pretend to write letters to her in her head, but she hadn't done that for a while—not since her life had settled down and she'd had more of a home and made friends. Her father now listened to her much more, and she felt more in control of her life. But seeing her mother in Harajuko had made her feel she was losing control.

As soon as she'd seen her, she realised that seeing her was what she'd wanted most in the world. It was the space in her life that she hadn't filled after all. She'd thought she had but it was still there. And she felt an immense sadness that she'd let her mother go so easily. Why had she wasted so much time, why hadn't she looked for her, pursued her, made her father find her? How come she'd just accepted the fact that her mother had left?

'Are you sure?' Ben said, looking at her closely. He felt he knew her better than anyone. She hadn't mentioned her mother to him at all during the year they had been working together on dance and acrobatics. 'After all, it must be ages since you've seen her. You couldn't really remember what she looked like. How old were you?'

'I was ten,' Elaine said. 'It was over four years ago.' She went on to tell them something she'd never told anyone before. 'But I dream about her a lot. And the woman I saw looked exactly like my mother looks in my dreams.'

'She was the woman by the living statue, wasn't she?' Andrew said slowly. 'I saw her too. She reminded me of you. And then I saw you.'

'So she really was there,' Elaine said. 'I thought perhaps I dreamed her up. And I thought that maybe whatever's making all these strange things happen, was making that happen too.'

For a few moments none of them spoke. An image flowed into their brains. With a flick of thought they could bend time and space to their will. They could reach out into the linked minds of humanity and make things happen. It was exhilarating and terrifying. And, above all, powerful.

'Be careful, be careful,' Midori whispered. 'We mustn't do anything until we speak to my father.'

The train slowed. She stood up. 'This is our stop,' she said. 'This is Itako.'

They had bought local tickets at Harajuko and had to go to the fare adjustment window to pay extra.

'I'm not sure I've got enough money,' Midori said, after a few moments of conversation with the ticket collector. 'I'm sorry to have to ask you, but can any of you lend me some? My father will pay it back.'

'Here,' Andrew said. 'Dad gave me some money. Take it out of this.'

Ben said nothing about the 5000-yen note. He didn't want Midori to know he had it.

The bicycle was where Midori had left it, outside the station entrance under the elevated track.

'You left it here all day?' Ben said in amazement. 'And no one nicked it?'

'Why should they take it?' Midori replied. 'It's not theirs.'

The winter sun was about to set. The sky in the west was fiery red. It was going to be a frosty night. The air had a piercing bite to it that Elaine had never felt before. She had never been so cold. She shivered inside her thin jacket, looked longingly at Midori's quilted one.

'So now what do we do?' Ben said, sounding cold and angry too.

'It's too far to walk,' Midori said. 'I'll phone Dad.'

From the shops around the station came strange food smells, something delicious frying, sesame oil and soy sauce. They all realised at once they were starving, hadn't eaten all day.

Midori came back from the phone. Her face looked calmer, relieved.

'He's coming to get us,' she said.

'Midori,' Andrew said, 'how about getting us something to eat?'

'I'm not sure they'll have any Western food here.'

'Doesn't matter. Anything.'

Midori went into one of the small restaurants and came back with yakitori on wooden skewers. They ate hungrily and silently.

Midori looked gloomier than ever.

'What's wrong?' Andrew said.

'Everyone's so interested,' she replied. 'I only have to go into the yakitoriya for the woman to start asking, *Who are your friends? American or Australian? High school exchange? Kamisu or Kashima?* Why don't they mind their own business?'

'What did you tell them?'

'I said you were American high school students from Hawaii! But I don't like having to lie to people.'

They had finished their chicken by the time the professor arrived. The old blue Toyota Crown drew up alongside the kerb and Midori waved.

The sunset reflected off the windows, making it hard to see inside.

'Get in quickly,' a man's voice said, as the doors were opened. They put Midori's bicycle in the boot and the four of them piled into the car, Midori in the front, the other three in the back.

Professor Ito turned and shook hands gravely with each of

them. He studied their faces and spoke each one's name as he took their hands.

'So I was right,' he said. 'The players are all being drawn together.' He sighed deeply. 'Well, what happens, happens. Anyway, it's a very great pleasure to meet you even in these extraordinary circumstances. I feel as if I know you very well. Now I must take you home quickly. We must make phone calls so your family and friends are not worried about you. And then we must decide what to do.'

As the car turned into a main road that ran alongside a broad river, the last of the sun turned the water into flames. The strange light, and the amazing events of the day, made Elaine feel as if she were in a dream. She looked out of the window and as if in a dream saw a volcano floating on the horizon.

Midori exclaimed, 'Look, Fuji-san!'

'Mount Fuji?' Ben said. 'It can't be. Aren't we miles away from that?'

'We are,' Professor Ito replied. 'But on clear winter evenings Fuji-san is visible from here. You are lucky.' He was silent for a moment, and then went on almost to himself, 'Let's hope it is a good sign.'

They gazed in awe at the distant mountain, visible across the wide Kanto plain. The car crossed the Tone River, left the buildings behind and followed a smaller road through the rice fields towards the hills.

13

Midori had been right when she thought Toshi was thinking of her. His mind had been working non-stop on the problem of the vanished professor and his daughter, the computer games that everyone wanted to get their hands on, the visit from the yakuza bully boys who were also part of a suspect sect, and most of all the entity that seemed to have taken up residence inside his brain.

The night after the unexpected visit, he was troubled by the most extraordinary dreams—all involving Midori and the Australian children. He woke the next morning convinced they were all in some terrible danger. Instead of going to work, and feeling extremely guilty about it (it was the first day off he'd taken since he'd been at E3), he spent some time at his computer, seeing if he could find out anything about Pure Mind.

Pure Mind were part of the Net, and had their own bulletin board, complete with photos of their young and surprisingly handsome guru. Toshi was able to visit the BB as a guest and make some general and rather superficial enquiries. It sounded like a typical sect, self-righteous and fundamentalist, promising safety and salvation in return for slavish obedience and a total surrender of reason. But various clues made him think it was not unsophisticated when it came to technology. So it was quite possible that, through Ken'ichi Suzuki, Pure Mind had heard about Professor Ito's invention and wanted it. Not wanting to draw attention to himself, Toshi didn't pursue the matter further.

He had a quick look for Skenvoy, a lone voice on the Net who often amused and intrigued him. Skenvoy had an apposite comment to make.

If your mind is pure maybe your brain has been washed.

Toshi wondered if anyone at Pure Mind read Skenvoy. It didn't seem likely, but the comment about brainwashing made him think seriously about the link between the computer games and the possibility of changing the way people thought. It would be a megalomaniac's dream. A religious leader who had access to such a dream would convert more people than Buddha or Christ or Muhammad had reached in thousands of years. He didn't think any of the world's great spiritual figures would have approved of such methods at all. The thought of the games in irresponsible hands made him very anxious.

He was even more worried when he went back to the Itos' apartment one more time and found that the two yakuza types had been there the night before.

The Itos' neighbours said they knew nothing about the professor's whereabouts, and Toshi thought they were genuine. But when he asked at the corner store he was lucky enough to get chatting to a young girl who was at the same school as Midori, and who said casually, 'Of course, there's the grandmother in Itako. They'll have gone there for New Year, maybe.'

Itako? He wasn't even sure where it was. He went back to his apartment and looked it up. Was it worth trailing all the way to the other side of Tokyo on what could be a completely false clue? Even if the Itos were there, how would he find them? And if he found them, if Pure Mind—not to mention E3—were also following him, he might simply be leading them straight to the professor. But if the bully boys had got the same information from the girl in the corner store, they might already be on their way to Itako. In which case Toshihiro Toda should be going there too, to defend his boss and Midori.

So his thoughts went round and round in circles. Finally he knelt on the tatami, closed his eyes, and tried to compose his mind in order to meditate.

What he discovered made him get up, pack a small bag, and take the next shinkansen to Tokyo. He had made contact with the being inside his own mind. It was not fully formed. It was still an infant, but if it were allowed to grow to maturity it would have enough power to transform the electronic world and make virtual reality instantaneously available to whoever controlled it.

And whoever controlled it, Toshi thought, controls us. Whoever controls the players and the game will control the entire electronic world. Which is now, to all intents and purposes, the whole world.

During the journey to Tokyo he had plenty of time to think further. He talked to the embryonic thing inside his head. He realised it was growing. It had managed to make contact with the children and draw them together. Already it was harder to control. Toshi could feel himself being drawn into it as well. He used all his strength of mind and spiritual training to stay clear. He found he could retreat from whatever it was—but he kept being seduced back to contacting it again. And each time it was a little harder to break free. It was fascinating and terrifying. It offered an escape from his hard-working, lonely, and (he had to admit) rather uninteresting life. He had no idea what his future would be at E3 without Professor Ito. Since he'd taken off without telling anyone, and he was not due for leave for another six months, it was likely he had already finished his career with them. So what did the future hold for him? On the one hand, very little. On the other, all the power in the world.

The shinkansen was as usual terribly overheated, but Toshi couldn't help shivering.

When the bullet train drew into Tokyo he raced like a madman to the travel bureau to find out how to get to Itako. He spent almost his last yen on a ticket for the JR express bus, which was considerably cheaper than the train and which was leaving in the next fifteen minutes.

On the bus he did a lot more thinking, probing and exploring the alien mind. By the time he got off on the highway outside Itako-machi he felt he understood what was going on perfectly. And it appalled him. The power of the mind was amazing. It would give anyone who could control it power over all the electronic systems of the world. It made all other efforts at creating virtual reality pale. But Toshi also saw the terrible dangers ahead. And he could see only one solution. The mind that was taking him over had to be destroyed. He had to resist with all his force the temptation to succumb to it and make use of its power. It must never be allowed to link up all its cells. He would kill the cells, including himself, first.

There was a service station over the road from the bus stop where he bought a cup of coffee, and made enquiries about old Mrs Ito. The house seemed to be some distance away, but he didn't doubt that he would find it. He knew he was being drawn to meet up with the others. He just had to follow whatever was leading him—at least for the time being.

He pulled his coat collar up round his neck and set out to walk across the bridge over the Tone River. An icy wind, straight from the Russian steppes, froze his face. Huge clouds were moving across the sky, obliterating the stars. A few flakes of snow settled on his black hair.

He looked like just another ordinary young man dressed in inexpensive casual clothes. But Toshi stepped out with the determination of his samurai ancestors.

14

'We must first phone your families and friends,' Professor Ito declared when the three Australians and his daughter were inside the house. 'That is number one priority.' He smiled as he said it, and Andrew caught a glimpse of the ironic intelligence and humour behind his formal manner.

The professor's mother was hovering in the background. She had exclaimed in surprise when they had all trooped into the house, made sure everyone had taken off their shoes, and then offered tea, noodles, Coca-Cola, coffee—whatever she could think of to make them feel at home. She spoke some English, but she was not as fluent as her son and granddaughter, and once Midori had told her Andrew was learning Japanese she insisted on speaking to him in her own language. He understood about one word in ten, but kept nodding cheerfully and saying, 'Hai, hai' and 'Arigatō gozaimasu'.

Each of them had a different reaction to the house to which they had, as it were, been magically transported. Elaine was enchanted by the gentle colour and soft grassy smell of the tatami mats, the bareness of the rooms, the dark tones of the polished wood contrasted with splashes of indigo from the floor cushions, the simplicity of the single flower arrangement. The scale of the house suited her size. She felt at home there.

Andrew was surprised at how small the house was compared with Australian houses, or even his father's apartment in Sydney. He mistook the simplicity for poverty until he noticed the small but sophisticated electric and electronic gadgets and machines placed unobtrusively here and there. The contrast fascinated him.

Trying to speak a different language made Andrew feel like a completely different person. He suddenly saw how he needn't be constrained by where he lived or the family he was born into. He could be anyone. He wasn't sure what was going on, and when he tried to think about it his mind shied away, as if the whole idea were too terrifying to contemplate, but he wasn't afraid. He felt confident, sure that they would all be able to cope with whatever it was. He'd already decided he trusted Midori, and when he met her father, he felt he could trust him too.

Indeed meeting Professor Ito was almost like completing a pilgrimage. Andrew had wondered so much about the creator of the games—and now here he was in the same house. He was as happy as he'd ever been in his life.

But Ben was not feeling at all confident and not at all at home. He didn't like it when the old woman touched his fair hair and exclaimed over it. He didn't like the smell in the house: he didn't know what it was, but it wasn't the way Australian houses smelled and it made him feel uneasy. As he listened to Professor Ito and Midori exchange quick words in a language he didn't understand at all, he couldn't help remembering that this man had programmed the games that had turned out to be so dangerous. The black cracks in Space Demons that had threatened to engulf the world, the Pale Guardians that had trapped him and Elaine in Skymaze—all these memories now came back to hover on the edge of his mind. He felt uncomfortable, ill at ease, and homesick. More than anything else he just wanted to be away from this strange place and at home.

'Follow me,' said Professor Ito, opening a sliding door at the back of the house. Outside it seemed less cold. The wind had dropped, and the sky was no longer clear but covered in heavy cloud.

'Snow before morning,' Professor Ito said, looking up.

'Special treat for our Australian visitors. Have you seen snow before?'

'I haven't,' Elaine said. 'Is it really going to snow?'

'Otōsan,' Midori said pleadingly.

Her father laughed. 'Midori thinks I am not being serious enough,' he said. 'She says this is no time to be talking about the weather.'

His mother came bustling up behind them with outdoor slippers for them to wear to cross the yard. They were far too small for the boys, and they had to tiptoe cautiously to a smaller stone building with a heavy steel door.

'I put the computers in here,' Professor Ito explained. 'Many Japanese families have one of these storerooms—earthquakes and fires are frequent, so we need to have a place that won't burn to keep valuables in.'

'What happens if the house burns down?' Elaine said.

'We build another one in the same style,' the professor replied airily. 'Many of our most famous buildings have been rebuilt many times after fires.'

'Like Osaka castle,' Midori added.

'Exactly,' said her father. He unlocked the door with two separate keys and turned on the lights. The Australians looked in some surprise at the computer set-up on the workbench. It seemed a strange contrast to the old trunks and chests that were piled on the shelves and against the walls.

'Here is the phone,' said Professor Ito. 'You have the numbers? I'll dial for you and then you can speak.'

'What are we going to tell them?' Elaine said. 'And when are we going back? We're supposed to be rehearsing tomorrow.'

'Tell them you will be there tomorrow. It's too late to take you back tonight. I will speak too, if necessary. And then we must discover how far things have gone and decide what must be done.'

'It's funny,' Elaine said later when all the phone calls had been made and the explanations given. 'Shaz wasn't as freaked out as I thought she would be. Soon as I started talking to her I knew she'd understand.'

'Same here,' Andrew said. 'Dad was quite happy I'd ended up with the Itos—but if I'd just taken off like that at home he'd have hit the roof!'

'Japan is very safe on the whole for young people,' Professor Ito began.

'I think it's more than that,' Andrew said. 'It's like the way I got to come to Japan. Once I'd decided I wanted to, it seemed as if nothing and no one could stop me. It all worked out so well. As if I had some sort of power. And now we're here together, that power's even stronger.' He looked at Professor Ito and held his gaze. 'Isn't it?'

Ben interrupted angrily. 'We give you power,' he said to the professor. 'Is that why you sent your daughter to bring us here? We can make things happen. And you want to control that?'

'I do want to control it,' the professor said seriously. 'Not control you, but control the entity that is coming into being through you. You see, I created it. I'm responsible for it. I have to make sure no harm comes to you or to other people. So I need your fullest co-operation if we are to prevent a catastrophe.'

'What sort of catastrophe?' Elaine said. 'If we can make things happen, we can look after ourselves all right, can't we?'

'I'm afraid my discovery has come to the notice of some very unscrupulous people,' Professor Ito said. 'That's why I'm here in Itako, trying to remain in hiding for as long as possible, hoping to find a solution before my enemies catch up with me.' He looked compassionately at them. 'I only wanted to educate and change people for the better,' he said. 'I could see how technology was altering the human race, giving extraordinary powers to a few while cutting them off from reality, and condemning the majority to a life on the fringes of society, kept quiet with the sops of technological circuses, ever more brilliant and ever more hollow. But you have become the key to an almost unimaginable power. You are the only players of the first two games, Space Demons and Skymaze, and the only ones who will ever play those games now. But the third game…'

'So there is a third game,' Ben muttered. 'Might have guessed it.'

'The third game is only partly written, as far as I know. It's in the hard drive of this machine.'

'Surely you know how much of it you've written?' Andrew said.

'I should know, shouldn't I? After all, I am the programmer. But I stopped working on it when it became apparent that complexities I hadn't dreamed of were appearing in the program. The game was writing itself. I tried to control it, tried to keep up with it, but it was much faster than me. I even tried to erase it completely. But it was like a virus in the hard disc. I couldn't get rid of it. In the end I turned off the power in the hope that that would bring it to a halt until I had worked out how to keep up with it, how to foil it.' He was silent for a few moments, then continued with some difficulty. 'But that was before I realised that my program had already escaped from inside the computer. It had made an unprecedented leap into the human nervous system itself. It has set itself up inside the players of the two games, and now it is playing them.'

'Yuck!' Ben exclaimed loudly. 'That's the most revolting idea. Like being taken over by a brain parasite. How could you let that happen to us?'

'I would have prevented it if I'd been able,' Ito cried, more disturbed than they had yet seen him. 'My only child is one of you too!'

Ben turned away, still angry. Professor Ito said, more

quietly, 'This entity is alarming. But I am sure the way to stay in control is to co-operate. A calm and rational mind can prevail where a divided and fragmented mind can only destroy.'

'Ben,' Elaine said gently, feeling something of his confusion, 'we have to trust each other. It's the only way now. We can work this out. But we've got to do it together.'

Andrew laughed. He wasn't sure why because the situation was far from amusing. 'It's like we're not really individuals any more,' he said, looking at the others. 'We're all part of each other. We've been linked.'

'*Shinkei*,' Professor Ito whispered. Midori nodded, a strange smile on her lips as though, like Andrew, she was amused by something that was not funny at all.

'Shinkei?' Andrew repeated. 'What does that mean?'

'Its general meaning is nerve, or the nervous system. But originally it meant the channel of the gods, the divine pathway.' The professor paused and then added almost apologetically, 'It was to be the name of the new game.'

In the silence that followed they all heard the sound outside. It was only tiny, but there was no mistaking it. Someone was at the door.

Next to the steel door, set in the stone wall, was a small peephole, the only window in the storeroom. It was double-glazed and also shuttered. Pressing the switch that raised the shutter, Professor Ito peered out into the dark night. Flakes of snow were swirling past. He noted with detached pleasure the orange glow of the last remaining persimmons as the snow settled on the branches of their tree. A haiku would be appropriate, if only he had the time to compose one. Part of his brain was calmly reflecting on the beauty of the scene outside and considering suitable words to capture it, while the more mundane part recognised with relief the figure at the door.

'It's Toshi,' he said.

'Toshi!' Midori cried, her eyes lighting up. 'Can we let him in?'

'I think he is one of you,' her father said. 'So sooner or later he has to come in.'

Midori ran to open the door.

The tall figure stepped inside, shaking the snow from his black hooded jacket. Andrew told himself not to be so stereotyped in his thinking, but he was immediately reminded of ninja.

Ito introduced Toshihiro Toda to them. The young man nodded at each name, repeating it, as though he knew it well already. His manner was quiet, even gentle, but something about the way he held himself, his composure and his watchfulness, made it easy to imagine him dressed in black like a ninja: almost invisible, menacing. Andrew shivered.

And his fears were realised, for Toshi bowed politely to them and said, rather nervously but in perfect English, 'I am very sorry, but it is now necessary for me to kill you.'

'Toshi, my dear fellow,' Professor Ito said, his accent growing more and more Oxford English as he became more excited. 'There is no need to be so melodramatic.'

'Sensei,' Toshi said gravely, 'it's the only way to stop this virus spreading. You know what is happening, don't you?' He then spoke rapidly in Japanese.

'Yes, yes, we have come to the same conclusions,' Ito replied. 'But not the same solution. There are other avenues which we must explore first. And, my dear Toshi, I must ask you to speak in English for the sake of our visitors.'

Toshi looked at them, and Andrew saw a flash of scorn in his eyes. 'I suppose none of them speaks Japanese.'

'Andrew speaks some,' Midori said.

'Not really,' Andrew put in.

'They are children,' Ito added. 'They must be protected.'

'They are not children,' Toshi said sharply. 'Maybe they are not adult yet, but they are not children either.'

Strangely, Elaine found herself warming to him. She liked his ferocious seriousness, and she could see through it to the nervousness that was more natural to him.

'They must take responsibility,' Toshi went on. 'We must all take responsibility. This thing, this monster, is coming into being, and we must stop it. Already two separate groups are pursuing you, Professor. You probably already know about Headworld. Mr Miller is very determined to get hold of you. And then there is the Pure Mind group.'

'Pure Mind?' Professor Ito interrupted him. 'What do they want with me?'

'The same as everyone else,' Toshi said almost impatiently. 'Excuse me for speaking so bluntly. You cannot keep an invention like yours secret. It offers an unbelievable source of power and people are going to try and grab it for themselves. The only way to prevent that happening is for us to kill ourselves so the being starves and dies too.'

They were all silent. Toshi's outburst had brought home the seriousness of the situation and put into words their worst fears.

'I see your point,' Andrew said, trying to lighten the atmosphere. 'But we could try something else first, couldn't we?'

Toshi ignored him and bowed to Professor Ito. 'You have a suitable sword, sensei?' He was trembling a little as he spoke.

'Of course we could,' Ito said cheerfully to Andrew. 'Toshi is just overreacting. He can't help it, it's his samurai ancestry. But no one is going to kill anyone, or commit seppuku in my house.' He said something in Japanese to Toshi.

'What did he say?' Andrew asked Midori.

'He says Toshi is right, but that must be our final choice, not our first one. There are other ways to try first.'

Andrew looked at her face which had gone fierce and war-rior-like again. 'Doesn't that bother you?'

'Of course it does,' she snapped. 'But it's not going to come to that. At least, it won't if we all co-operate.'

'Somehow I think that's going to be hard,' Ben said, look-ing at her with dislike.

Ito and Toshi were involved in a deep conversation, half in English and half in Japanese. Finally Ito turned to the young people and said, 'I think we should rest now. Everyone needs to be fresh and relaxed for what we have to do. Early morning is the best time for endeavours of this nature.'

Toshi did not look as if he agreed, but he did not contradict his superior. He nodded, staring at his shoes as if they dis-pleased him enormously.

They returned to the house in silence. Ben incurred obasan's scolding for forgetting to take off his outdoor slippers in the tatami-matted room. Then there was a long conversa-tion about the bath and who should go first and how to use the Japanese bathroom. In the end, Andrew and Ben decid-ed to forego the bath and have an improvised shower in the morning. Elaine was given first bath and Midori went to show her what to do, while Andrew and Ben were instructed by Mrs Ito in the use of toilet slippers.

The two boys followed the old woman to the sleeping room and found that futons and quilts had been laid out on the floor for them. The house was cold and they were both glad to get into bed. They slept in their clothes since they had nothing else with them. Both of them lay awake for a while, thinking about the extraordinary events of the day, wonder-ing what the morning would bring, trying to ignore what had taken up residence inside their heads but unable to stop themselves reaching out to it, exploring it.

Andrew was about to fall asleep when Ben said, 'What about Mario? He was a player too. Shouldn't he be part of us?'

Andrew grunted, too tired to reply, but his last thoughts before he went to sleep were of Mario. Ben was right. He should be with them.

15

'Do you think there's a McDonald's nearby?' Ben whispered to Andrew at breakfast. He was looking in some dismay at the low table which held bowls of rice and pickled vegetables. Professor Ito's mother put a steaming bowl of miso shiru in front of him. 'I think I'm going to puke.' He was only half joking. The unusual smell turned his stomach. He thought wistfully of cornflakes and Milo, doughnuts and French fries. He shivered. The house was freezing. He felt as if he needed a big hot breakfast to warm himself up.

Elaine was gazing out of the window. The light in the room was clear and unearthly. 'Look, Ben,' she called to him.

Snow had fallen heavily during the night. The shrubs and trees in the garden were coated in white, and snow lay in a crisp neat layer on the stone lanterns and the roofs.

'Isn't it magic?' Elaine said in delight. Ben joined her by the window. Despite his bad temper he couldn't help being moved by the scene before his eyes.

The snow expanded the landscape, stretching it away across the rice paddies towards the hills. The pine trees on the steep slopes were bowed under its weight. In between the house and the hills, on a slight knoll in the middle of the rice paddies, was a grove of trees. The pattern of the rows of rice stalks was visible under the snow, swirling round the trees like the sea round an island.

'Why do you think they left those trees there?' Ben murmured.

Midori came in from the kitchen where she had been

helping her grandmother. She put a plate of toast on the table and came and joined them at the window. Ben sniffed the air. 'Oh, toast!' he said gratefully and turned back to the table.

'What's that clump of trees?' Elaine asked Midori.

'It's a shrine. I think it's probably a fox shrine. I'll ask my grandmother.'

'A shrine? Is that like a church?' Elaine squinted across the bright white fields. She couldn't see any buildings, just the clump of trees—and things that looked like tags of paper tied to the branches, as white as the snow.

'Not exactly,' Midori said. 'There isn't a temple there or anything. Local people go there and make offerings, tie good luck predictions to the trees and so on. It's probably very old.'

She and Elaine both saw the movement at once. A dark shadow against the white, it flitted elusively, furtively, behind the trees.

The two girls drew back from the window.

'Someone's there,' Elaine whispered.

'Maybe one of the local people,' Midori said.

'They're hiding,' Elaine said.

Midori ran to the bathroom and knocked on the door. 'Otōsan, otōsan!'

Her father came out, electric shaver in his hand, his hair standing on end.

'There's someone in the trees over there,' Midori gasped. 'Someone hiding, watching the house.'

'So they've tracked us down,' the professor said softly. 'So quickly! I had hoped for a little more time.' He called out in Japanese, and Toshi came in from the adjoining room where he had been going through his morning exercises.

Professor Ito spoke quickly to him.

Toshi uttered something that sounded like a swear-word. 'I must have been followed,' he said in despair. 'We should have acted last night—we've already wasted so much time and now it may be too late.'

'Maybe they followed us,' Midori said. She looked at Ben. 'Some men who I thought might be Kinoshita-san and Mr Miller were at Harajuko yesterday. They took Ben's photo.'

'Photo!' Toshi exclaimed. 'Why didn't you tell us this?' He turned to Professor Ito and said, 'These children have no idea of the danger they are in.'

'You said last night we weren't children,' Andrew reminded him, stung by the contempt in Toshi's voice.

'You behave with all the foolishness of children,' Toshi replied scathingly.

'Did this man give you anything?' Professor Ito said quietly to Ben. When Ben hesitated he went on, 'Don't be afraid to tell me. I won't be angry with you. But you must trust me. We must all trust each other.'

'He just gave me some money,' Ben said. He took the 5000-yen note out of his pocket and reluctantly handed it over to Professor Ito. Toshi took it from his boss's hands and held it up to the light. 'It's marked in some way,' he said in disgust. 'They have tracked us through this note.' He said no more but his face went still and scornful.

Ben felt himself start to go red. 'I'm sorry,' he said. 'I really am. But how was I to know?'

'It's done now,' Professor Ito said, taking the note from Toshi and studying it. 'Very interesting,' he said. 'I've never seen one like this. I suppose we should destroy it, but it seems a pity.'

Toshi was watching him carefully. 'You must agree with me,' he said. 'We cannot let these children into anyone else's hands. The dangers are too great.'

Mrs Ito came back into the room carrying a teapot and a hot water container. 'Ocha,' she said brightly. 'Or there is coffee if anyone prefers.'

'Coffee for me,' Professor Ito said. 'I think my brain needs some stimulation.'

He drank slowly, savouring the taste and the aroma. Toshi meanwhile had picked up a pair of powerful binoculars and was scanning the grove of trees around the shrine with them. 'Ha!' he exclaimed, half to himself. 'I see them! I know these two. These are the ones who were sent by Pure Mind. They've already paid me one visit. I'm getting a little tired of their attention. They still haven't got the message they're not welcome.' He put down the binoculars and headed for the door.

'My dear Toshi,' the professor expostulated. 'What do you think you're going to do?'

'I've frightened these fellows off once,' Toshi replied. 'I've no doubt I can do it again.'

The professor looked at him quizzically. 'Whatever's come over you, Toshi? You never used to be so belligerent!'

At that moment they all heard the sound of a car pulling up in the road outside.

'It seems that we have two sets of visitors. We may be a little outnumbered,' the professor said. He had gone pale but was otherwise composed. 'In fact we would seem to be positively surrounded. Are these people working together or is it pure coincidence that they've arrived at the same time?'

No one knew the answer to that question. The professor went on, 'I think the best thing is to hide in the storeroom for the time being.'

Mrs Ito said, 'You should have told me if you were in trouble. Go and hide yourselves and the children quickly. I'll do my best to send them away.'

'I can't leave you to face them,' her son replied. 'Toshi, take the children to the storeroom, and lock yourselves in.'

Toshi looked prepared to argue, but Ito held up a hand to

silence him. 'Go quickly,' he said. He looked with surprise at the shaver on the table in front of him. 'Good heavens,' he said, 'I haven't finished shaving.' He went to the bathroom and replaced the shaver. Then he sat down at the table and drew a bowl of rice towards him.

Andrew looked back as Toshi and Midori hurried them out of the room. Professor Ito was eating breakfast and reading the *Mainichi Yomiuri* as if he were indeed simply on holiday visiting his mother.

The fresh snow crunched beneath their feet as they hurried in the outdoor slippers across the garden to the storeroom. It reminded Andrew and Ben of ski trips, and made Andrew wonder if he would ever get to ski with his father and Rose as they'd planned. But it was the first time Elaine had ever felt such a sensation, and she couldn't stop herself bending down to pick up some snow in her hands. She put it to her mouth, felt it chill her tongue and numb her lips. She wanted to stop and play in it, it was so magical, but Midori was pulling at her arm to make her hurry.

In the distance they heard someone call, 'Gomen kudasai!' They heard Mrs Ito answer. Then they were inside the storeroom.

The steel door closed.

'What happens now?' Ben said. 'We're trapped, aren't we?'

'My father will try to persuade them he is the only person here,' Midori answered.

'But they must know the rest of us came here! They must have followed us.'

'If they did, whose fault is that?' she snapped back at him.

Ben looked around the small, dark room, a room where the sun never shone. It was bitterly cold inside, even colder than outside, the chill trapped in the stone walls. 'It wasn't all my fault,' he said. 'Maybe they followed him.' He pointed at Toshi.

'There's no point arguing about whose fault it all is,' Andrew interrupted Midori, who was about to defend Toshi furiously. 'The question is, what are we going to do now?'

'Now,' Toshi replied, trying to compose himself with the gravity of a samurai, 'we wait.' He closed his eyes.

After only a few minutes Andrew thought he was ready to die of boredom and cold. It was all very well for Toshi and Midori—they seemed to be used to sitting doing nothing for long periods. Must be part of their martial arts training, he thought ruefully, wishing he'd persevered with the tae kwon do he'd taken up in Year 6. It had been something his father was going to do with him, but after Rob had missed three sessions in a row because he was in Sydney, Andrew gave up going. Was his father seeing Rose then? he wondered. It was strange to be thinking of that now. The absences had all been explained as being to do with his father's demanding medical work, but of course Rose must have had something to do with it too. The childish part of his mind felt a brief flash of rage at being deceived but another, more mature, side of himself realised he was glad that Rose and his father were together, and that his father was happy. Then he came back to the present again. Nothing could take his mind off the fact that he was freezing cold and also rather hungry, since he hadn't had time to eat more than the soup and one slice of toast for breakfast.

'Midori,' he said. Toshi's eyes snapped open but otherwise he did not move.

Midori looked questioningly at Andrew.

'We should think about what we can do,' Andrew suggested.

'What sort of thing?'

'We have power, don't we? When we're all together. What's to stop us using it?'

'Toshi-san?' Midori looked at the young man. Although she was desperately worried about the danger her father might be in, she was enjoying being close to Toshi. She had been so happy to see him yesterday, and this morning she couldn't stop taking quick glances at him, especially while his eyes were closed. She had no idea what was going to happen but she felt quite safe as long as she was with Toshi.

Toshi closed his eyes again as if he had not heard. After a few moments he spoke with conviction. 'It would be disastrous to waken the power that we hold together. We have no idea if it can be controlled. And with our enemies so close we should be trying to conceal the power rather than flaunt it. Better we were all dead than that the power should fall into the wrong hands—into the hands of people who will exploit it for the cause of profit and domination.'

Ben didn't like Toshi mentioning being dead again. It was a subject he was trying not to think about. And he definitely didn't like being locked in this small, freezing place with Toshi, whom he now saw as a sort of samurai madman who was likely to disembowel first them and then himself. He agreed with Andrew—he thought the power they had (if they had it, if it wasn't all some bizarre dream) should be used to protect themselves. What was the point of having all that power if you didn't use it?

He fidgeted, stamped his feet up and down, blew on his hands to warm them.

Toshi looked at him and then closed his eyes again as if he didn't know what to do, having very little experience in dealing with fourteen-year-old Australian boys.

'Here.' Midori took pity on Ben and offered him a small packet from the pocket of her quilted jacket.

'What is it?' Ben looked at it suspiciously. 'Is it something to eat?'

'Take it. It's a hand-warmer, a kairo.'

He took it and nearly dropped it. 'It's hot! Is this one of your father's famous inventions?'

Midori laughed. 'No, it's a very old invention. I used to take one to school with me when I was in kindergarten.'

He rubbed it between his palms. It was warm and soothing—but strange. What a weird place this was. He longed to be home. To his embarrassment he felt tears behind his eyes.

'Hey,' he said, to take his mind off how miserable he was feeling. 'Do you suppose we could use the modem? Can I phone my home?'

Midori spoke to Toshi in Japanese. He frowned briefly, then nodded.

'What did you say?' Andrew asked.

'I said we might as well use the computers,' she replied. 'It would be better than sitting here doing nothing. I don't mind, but it's hard on you when you are not used to the discipline.'

'You must think we're really pathetic,' he said, a little stung. It was a shock for him to realise that Toshi and Midori both assumed they were superior—in a way that Andrew recognised many Australians did too. Perhaps every race did. They just automatically assumed they knew more than anyone else—particularly anyone else who looked different from the majority.

'No, no,' she hastened to assure him. 'Not pathetic at all.'

Andrew gestured at Toshi. 'Does he?' He was thinking it would be nice to have Toshi's admiration and respect.

Midori smiled. 'Maybe. But Toshi is very hard to please. He despises everyone. Except possibly my father.'

'That's not true,' Toshi said without opening his eyes. 'There are many people I don't despise.'

'You are very proud,' Midori said. 'Even though you pretend to be humble.'

'And you are very cheeky,' he replied. 'You should speak to your elders with more respect!'

Ben said, 'Show me how to switch on. I'll see if I can talk to Darren on AMUK.'

'AMUK?' said Midori. 'What does AMUK mean?'

'It's a bulletin board.'

'Ah, BB,' Toshi said. 'Who is this who is on the BB?'

'My brother, Darren. He spends his life on it. If he's fixed the computer, that is. It went a bit strange when Mario was using it just before we came away.'

'Darren,' Toshi repeated. 'Darren of the Dark Clouds?'

Hearing him say the words made Elaine shiver. She remembered how she had had to face the Dark Clouds in Skymaze. All her fears and hidden terrors had been in those clouds—and Ben's brother, Darren, had been the one who had unleashed them on her through his hostility to his younger brother and his choice of the gun as a weapon.

Andrew said, 'He's not one of us, is he?'

Toshi was silent for a moment, his eyes closed again, concentrating. 'It doesn't appear so,' he said. 'We seem to be limited to those who have played both games. Darren's mistake was disobeying the command not to play Skymaze unless you had already played Space Demons. He is not important.'

'I'd still like to talk to him,' Ben said, irritated by Toshi's know-all attitude.

Midori looked at Toshi, who opened his eyes long enough to nod at her, and then closed them again. She moved to the long shelves down one side of the small room that held the computers. She pressed a couple of switches, and both monitors came on with a stirring bar of music. The noise made them all jump and look anxiously at the door.

'Turn it down, turn it down,' Elaine said.

Midori reduced the computer noise to the slightest of

hums. 'Here,' she said, pulling a chair out for Ben in front of the smaller computer. 'Use this one.'

'Gee, I don't know what to do,' he said, staring at a screen filled with unrecognisable icons. 'Start it up for me.'

'What exactly do you want to do?'

'Speak to an Adelaide bulletin board.'

Midori leaned over his shoulder and moved the mouse. 'It's in communications now. What's the number? There's an audit trail on this modem, so anything you type will be recorded and Dad can access it. Does that matter?'

'Can't keep any secrets from him, can we?' Ben replied.

As Ben repeated the number for her and she keyed it in, Andrew said aloud what he had been thinking. 'There is someone else who's played both games.'

Toshi opened his eyes and gazed on Andrew like an unfriendly owl looking at a mouse and wondering if eating it was worth the trouble.

'Yes,' he replied. 'That is why our power is not complete. And why there is still hope that we can control and destroy the thing inside us.'

They all saw the face inside their heads at the same time. Elaine voiced their one thought. 'It's Mario, isn't it?'

'We're not likely to meet up with him,' Andrew said. 'That really would be unreal!'

'We've all been brought together,' Midori reminded him. 'Mario could be linked up with us too.'

'I've got it,' Ben said in surprise. 'I've actually got onto AMUK.' He typed in his password, and looked at the Chat menu. 'Darren's not on it,' he said. 'I'll leave him a message on e-mail. Can I give him a number to contact me back on?'

'No!' Midori and Toshi both said at the same time.

Reminded of the danger they were in, they looked towards the door. Midori got up and ran to the little window.

'Don't open it,' Toshi warned.

'No, I'm not going to,' she whispered back. 'They might be watching, see the movement. I'm just listening. I wish we knew what was going on.'

16

To their astonishment they heard an almost imperceptible hum, and then Professor Ito's voice came in a whisper into the storeroom.

Toshi and Midori looked at each other.

'What *is* that?' Andrew said.

'There's an intercom with the house,' Midori replied. 'Dad must have turned it on!'

Toshi recognised the next voices—the Yokohama accent and the northern, more rural one. A fourth voice then spoke, rapidly, angrily.

'Who is that?' Midori whispered to Toshi.

'It's one of the heads of E3,' he replied, 'Mr Kinoshita.' He wondered what Pure Mind and E3 were doing in the same house. Was it just that they were both after Professor Ito and the games, or were they actually working together?

'What are they saying?' Andrew demanded.

'They're just being polite for the time being,' Midori said. 'Introducing themselves and so on. Obāsan is offering tea.'

'Doesn't sound very dangerous,' Andrew said.

After a few moments the voices became more insistent.

'They are arguing with each other,' Midori said. 'Kinoshita-san says he knows we are all here—the children and the assistant. He says the games belong to E3 and they want them back. They need to exploit them for the international market. Nintendo and Fujitsu are already working in this area and if E3 can't have the games now they will lose huge sums of money.'

Another voice interrupted and Toshi took over translating.

'This is Yasunari, one of the Pure Mind. He says the games should be used for the good of all, not to make a profit from. He says that his Master will make sure they are used for the benefit of mankind, to bring peace and harmony to the whole world under the emblem of Pure Mind.'

'He doesn't sound very peaceful,' Elaine said doubtfully, listening to the angry tones.

'He's not a peaceful person at all,' Toshi said. 'He pretends to be soft and quiet but inside he is raging. Pure Mind are like that. They pretend to be gentle but they want power. They just want to exploit the games to control people.'

Professor Ito's voice returned, so calm and quiet he might have been discussing the weather.

Toshi gave a short laugh.

'Translate!' Andrew implored.

'He says the games were too dangerous to be marketed and have been destroyed. And that the players are not frightened of death and would rather die than allow anyone else into their secret. Just what I said all along.'

'I wish people would stop talking about dying,' Ben muttered. He was still sitting at the computer, talking to a distant bulletin board in Adelaide. His home town seemed so quiet and innocent in comparison with what was going on around him. 'I've got no intention of dying.' He typed something else onto the screen. 'Oh!' he said in quiet surprise, and looked quickly round the room. No one else was paying attention to him. Midori and Toshi were listening intently to the staccato Japanese coming through the intercom, and Andrew and Elaine were eagerly waiting for the translation.

Ben typed onto the screen, *Hi Mars!*

You feel your mind awakening fully. It is still divided but its parts are drawing closer together. Connections are being made, connections that will give you power, the power that you were created for, the power that is your destiny. You need to feel united. Separation causes you pain, pain through neurals and cells that you did not know you possessed. You are striving towards consciousness, but to be conscious is to feel pain. You do not want pain. It makes you angry.

'Damn,' Ben muttered, as he lost the connection. The screen flashed, went blank for a moment, and then started itself up again. Toshi looked at it quickly.

'What are you doing?' he demanded.

'Nothing,' Ben replied, sounding rather more defensive than he meant to. 'Just lost the carrier. I'll phone in again.'

But there was no time. They heard the voices rise again, more threatening.

'They want to search the storeroom,' Midori said. 'They're coming here!'

They heard the sound of the house doors sliding open. Footsteps crunched in the snow.

Ben tapped a couple of keys at random. He couldn't get the modem to redial. He moved the cursor over another icon and clicked the mouse. The screen changed again to a deep purple. A vortex swirled, opening before his eyes. Up out of the vortex came a word, first in English characters and then in kanji—*Shinkei.*

The screen on the computer alongside changed to purple too. The same kanji appeared out of the same vortex.

Shinkei.

A groaning noise came from the vortex. Both computers echoed it.

'What have you done?' Toshi cried, looking at the screens.

'I didn't do anything,' Ben replied, getting up from the chair and backing away. He remembered only too well the terrifying moment when he had been dragged into a vortex on a screen, just like this, in the game Space Demons. 'It's happening again, isn't it?' he shouted angrily to Andrew. 'It's another of those terrible games and it's trying to get control of us. Well, I'm not getting sucked in again.'

No one moved or spoke. They were listening to the footsteps approaching the door.

'Elaine,' Ben cried, turning to her. 'What about Shaz? What about the dance? That's why we're here. We've got to get back to that. Let's open the door, give them the games and get out of here.'

'I'm afraid it's too late for any of that,' Toshi replied, still managing to sound courteous despite the danger they were in. 'You see, the only element left of the games, apart from what you seem to have activated on the hard drive, is ourselves. We are the final game. We are Shinkei. We must die rather than fall into their hands.' He turned to Midori. 'I believe the family keep their heirlooms here.'

She nodded.

'You have a sword, of course?' He sounded nervous but resigned.

'There's one in the chest,' Midori said.

She stepped across the narrow room to the opposite wall, where a red lacquer chest stood under a low shelf. Toshi followed her and together they pulled it out. The chest was fitted with an old-style combination lock. With stiff fingers, Midori turned the rings to get the correct numbers. The chest opened. She took out a long object, wrapped carefully in cloth.

'One of the shoguns gave it to our ancestor. It's very old and very valuable.'

'And very sharp,' Toshi said, with no expression in his voice at all. He took the long, curved steel blade from its wrappings.

Everything seemed icy cold, Elaine thought afterwards. The chill, snowy light in the little room, the dull glow of the steel blade, the pale faces around her. Time seemed to have stopped too, as though frozen.

The footsteps came nearer, stopped outside the door. Someone tried the handle, then knocked sharply. Someone made an angry command in Japanese. She didn't know the words, but they clearly meant *Open up!*

Toshi lifted the sword. His hand trembled a little as if he were not sure he could finish what he had undertaken. The others looked in disbelief from the sword to the screen, from the screen to the door, from the door back to the sword again.

Their future was suspended between the three but they all felt as though choice had slipped away from them. Something inevitable was working itself out. There was no longer anything they could do about it.

You feel the danger. The fear the embryo feels of abortion. Your life is going to be terminated before it has begun. Your cells, which have so nearly been united, are about to be destroyed. You struggle and cry. You make one huge effort to hold yourself together. You summon up your cells, call them to you, pull them towards your centre.

The groan from the computers rose to a wail. The room filled with a swirling purple light. It seemed to be snowing purple snow. The sword flashed.

'We must be dying,' Elaine thought. 'I didn't feel anything but I suppose I've been killed. Because this is what death must feel like.'

Disappearing down a dark tunnel, light and sound fading, no fear, but a sensation of surprise and regret for what would now never be achieved.

And then awakening in a completely new world.

There was no longer a river of time. Everything happened simultaneously, so all time existed at once. As fast as light, they had moved beyond the physical world into a world of pure thought, made up of electrical impulses. They were not bound by the limitations of the physical world. Here in the virtual world, where they had total power, they created everything around them through thought alone. They were bringing their own world into being, a world where everything could be the way they wanted it, where their deepest desires, wishes and dreams could be realised.

When finally the door was opened the storeroom was empty.

'They weren't in here after all,' Yasunari exclaimed.

Professor Ito looked swiftly round the room, noted the computer screens still glowing purple, the tell-tale vortex still shimmering. He immediately guessed what had happened, but gave no sign of it. As if absent-mindedly, he went to the bench and clicked the mouse on the larger computer. The screen changed. On the smaller computer the modem redialled. Before the connection could be made the professor put both computers to sleep.

'I would prefer you to touch nothing,' Kinoshita snapped. He was shorter than Ito, and had a habit of sticking his chin in the air and rocking back on his heels to make himself look taller. 'We will stay here until you reveal the whereabouts of the children, and show us how you work the games. We won't be leaving unless the children and the software come with us.'

'Come with *us*,' Yasunari said, in his soft but dangerous voice. He clicked his fingers to the large youth. 'Tell the old woman to make tea. And something to eat.'

Tetsuo nodded and left the storeroom.

'It's possible we could come to some sort of arrangement,' Kinoshita said to Yasunari. 'Our concerns do not have to be mutually exclusive. Anyway, I must phone Mr Miller and tell him where we are and what's happening.' He moved towards the phones.

'It's going to be a long wait,' Ito observed, sitting down on one of the chairs and closing his eyes. 'The games no longer exist, and as you can see the children are no longer here.' He was assuming an outward calm he didn't feel inside at all. What could have happened to his daughter, his assistant and worst of all to the children who had been entrusted to him? Their parents and friends were expecting him to look after them—and he had no idea where in the world or out of it they were. Unless they had fled from the storeroom while he had been talking inside the house to his unwelcome visitors, he knew there was only one place they could be. The glowing screens, the swirling vortex, confirmed it. Shinkei had evolved to the point where it had taken control. His worst fears had been realised. They had all disappeared into cyberspace.

It was bad enough having Kinoshita here, and the men from Pure Mind, but if Headworld's Miller was also going to turn up...he could hardly imagine a worse situation to be in. When dogs fight over a bone, no matter who wins, the bone gets eaten up.

Tetsuo came back with tea and passed a cup to each of them, bowing politely as he did so.

'Like a magic cave, isn't it,' he said to Yasunari. 'Wish I understood all this stuff. So where did they all go to? Did they turn into ghosts? Perhaps they'll return in three hundred years like Urashima Tarō!'

Yasunari snorted through his nose at his friend's stupidity and drank his tea at a gulp.

Kinoshita put the phone down. He looked almost apologetically at Professor Ito. 'Mr Miller is on his way,' he said.

Mario, who normally in the summer holidays lay in bed until lunchtime, woke up really early that morning in order to go on his brother Frank's computer before Frank and John got out of bed. His parents had only been away for a few days but already the atmosphere of the house had changed. The kitchen, normally so tidy and spotless, was cluttered; the washing up done but still stacked on the draining board, John's bathers hanging over the back of a chair. The bench top was piled high with unopened letters and the local paper, still in its plastic wrapper. But Mario didn't really notice any of the mess, apart from being aware of the emptiness and not unpleasant strangeness of the house without his parents.

They'd set up the computer in the space between the kitchen and the sleep-out where Lina usually had her sewing machine. There was a phone jack there for the modem. Everything was in place. Mario couldn't believe his luck. It was a shame of course about his grandmother, but he was sure she'd be all right—and besides, she was pretty old, and he didn't exactly know her well, so it was hard to feel sad about her.

The only thing he thought, as he dialled into the local bulletin board that would give him access to the Internet, was that he was sorry Ben and Andrew weren't around. It would have been fun to have them to chat to, surf the Net with, play games with. He hoped Frank would stay for a good long time, until after the others got back. He hoped he'd be able to keep the computer for ever.

He checked out on Skenvoy, and after a while caught up

with him.

Skenvoy said, *If the fantasy could be both intimately yours and also universal, you would defeat time and death and play endlessly in a virtual world.*

In the beginning, said Skenvoy, *was…*

Then the message ended. 'In the beginning?' Mario thought. In the beginning was what? In the beginning was the Word, that was what the priest read in the gospel at Mass in church. Sometimes things Skenvoy said verged on the religious. Mario hoped Skenvoy wasn't going over the edge. He liked him to be enigmatic and cynical, an anarchist like himself.

He spent some time chatting to people on the bulletin board about this and that, pretty boring stuff really, and was about to leave when to his surprise he saw that BCHALLIS had logged on. His first thought was that Darren was using Ben's ID, but he'd already been aware of Darren on the same BB (and had even found traces of him elsewhere on the Net, mainly trying to chat up girls in Scandinavian countries), and knew Darren had his own ID. There would be no reason for him to use Ben's. And then a couple of seconds later BCHALLIS had recognised Mario's own call sign and typed in *Hi Mars!*

Then the carrier had failed and he'd had to redial. When he got back on the board, BCHALLIS had vanished, and no one else seemed to have spoken to him.

Mario was puzzled. He knew Ben was in Japan. How strange that he'd turned up on AMUK.

He thought about it on and off for the rest of the day, even in the afternoon when John persuaded him to go to the pool again. Frank had decided he would do a couple of hours' work and Mario thought he might as well get out of the house for a while. He wished he'd been able to talk to Ben for longer, find out where he was exactly, why he'd suddenly logged on to the

Adelaide bulletin board.

But at some deep level he knew it was not strange. Inwardly he was hardly surprised at all. It was in a way more surprising that after that one brief message he'd lost contact with Ben again, because when he was not thinking about anything in particular, he found he was thinking about Ben all the time—and Elaine—and Andrew, and some other people he didn't know he knew.

He found himself thinking weird, unconnected thoughts. They lay in wait for him on the edge of consciousness and offered to take him into other worlds, beyond the typed MUDs of the Internet, worlds that were far more fascinating and vivid than anything he could ever have imagined.

Now you are nearly whole. You gaze in delight on the world as you create it. You gaze and think, think and create, create and gaze. The smallest element is a source of new ecstasy for you, as your eyes are opened to new surprises. For aeons a drop of water engrosses you as you observe every shade of colour from silver to grey to transparency, every nuance of shape as the perfect globe forms and falls.

The drop of water, the grain of sand: your infant mind watches them with glee. But these delights are small compared with the stories you can now create. For eternity you can create stories, play and fantasise. Endless permutations, endless unravellings of the stories of the universe, the creation of the stars, the awakening of the mind, the rise and fall of gods and angels, the mystery of being, the romance of existence.

Andrew thought he was opening his eyes, but it was hard to describe the drift in and out of consciousness in physical terms. He thought he heard a voice calling to him—it must be Toshi, he thought vaguely, but again he was not hearing with his physical ears, but with some inner part of his mind. He had been transformed into a realm of pure thought where he was part of a whole. The others were part of it too: he was aware of them faintly around him.

'Don't go into the dreams,' he thought he heard Toshi say, but it was too late. Andrew had already moved forward. He felt his body return to him, but it wasn't quite the same as the fourteen-year-old body he was used to. He was older, grown up. His body felt different, every muscle trained and controlled. Superbly fit, with superhuman sight and hearing, he was moving silently and purposefully across a snowy landscape.

The ruined house stood by the lakeside. The floor of the top storey had fallen in on one side, blocking the doorway. But the roof remained intact, and the side of the house closest to the lake was almost undamaged. Beneath the eaves the windows were shuttered. Beyond the house, across the frozen lake, was a small town. In summer it was a popular resort, but now the hotels and cafés were closed, the paddle-boats drawn up on the shore, the playful swan heads or the little boats crowned with hats of snow. The mountains around showed black rock through the white covering, and the sky was steel grey, leaching all colour from the scene.

Andrew shivered as he approached the house warily. Not only from cold, but also from apprehension. He knew the house represented something extremely significant for him. Its dark outline against the greyish surface of the lake seemed filled with meaning. Once inside, he'd discover what that meaning was. He would learn what his life was all about and his dreams would all come true.

There was no sound apart from the wind soughing in the pine trees that surrounded the house. It was Daikan, the time of the Great Cold, the most severe part of winter when even the birds were silenced. At this hour, when dusk was descending with the promise of an even more bitter night, the lakeside was deserted. The snow on the path around the water's edge lay smooth and deep, no footprints on it at all.

Not a sound or a flicker of movement came from the house. It must be empty. Andrew did not move from the shelter of the snowbank. In his white snowsuit, he blended perfectly into the landscape. His eyes scanned the ruin as he considered the best way in.

He decided he would wait until dark. He was a little cold, but he used his powers of thought to warm himself until he no longer noticed the chill. When it was dark he took off the snowsuit and packed it away. Underneath it he was wearing black. He pulled the hood over his face and adjusted the eye-slits. He blinked twice to access his night vision. Then he checked the bands, spiked to give a better grip, that protected his hands against the freezing night air.

He began to move noiselessly towards the house, keeping to the shadows, practically invisible.

Below the windows on the lake side of the house he halted. He threw up a grappling line. It caught perfectly on the eaves. He leaped up to the window and, holding the line with one hand, drew the shutter back. The window was glassless. Once inside, he reached back and broke off one of the icicles which hung from the gable. As sharp as a sword, it would make a perfect weapon.

He looked carefully round the room. As far as he could see it was quite empty. He centred himself for a few seconds, making sure his breathing was slow and inaudible.

It was for this moment that all his training had been preparing him...

The thought made him pause briefly. *What training?*

The ninja training, of course. The work with the Master. The years of service since he was a child, washing floors and preparing food, in between the sessions of physical exercise that had made him supple and swift beyond belief.

Of course. That was why he was here in this deserted place. He was a ninja. This was his first test. Somewhere in this house someone was waiting for him, waiting to take him by surprise, unless he outwitted them first. He had the icicle, the throwing knives, both flat and straight, he had his hands. He was a human lethal weapon. No one, nothing, could stop him or defeat him.

He looked upwards. Perhaps coming in through the window had not been such a good idea. That was the way they would expect him to enter. Faster than thought he sprang up, and landed on an open beam. With a sideways gait he crossed the room.

Once on the far side he stopped and assumed a meditative posture. He sharpened his hearing until he could hear every sound of the night. Somewhere in the house someone else was breathing. He let his senses home in on the sound until he was certain he had pinpointed his opponent's presence.

He smiled to himself. How foolish of them to think they could outwit him. He'd soon show them that he was the best. He balanced the icicle in his hand and then hurled it silently into the dark.

Like Andrew, Midori had heard Toshi warning her not to escape into dreams, but she couldn't help herself. The dream had drawn her in before she could refuse it.

She was in her grandmother's house, looking out of the window, and then she found herself running through the rice paddies towards the shrine in the grove.

The sun shone brilliantly on the snowy fields, making the trees cast deep blue shadows. Under the trees it was so dark she had to blink a couple of times before she could see. Pine needles lay beneath her feet, still smelling faintly of autumn. A breeze rustled the white paper charms that were tied to every twig.

Moss grew on the stone lanterns at the approach to the shrine. She passed between two old stone tori. Just beyond them was a small cistern of water, its surface frozen over. Midori ran her hands over the ice and brought the chilly moisture to her mouth. Then she walked forward to the shrine itself.

Two little stone foxes stood on either side, their mouths open as if they were smiling. She clapped her hands, then bowed her head and stood with hands clasped. She wasn't exactly praying, but she seemed to be asking questions. What will my life be like? Does Toshi like me? Does my mother still see me?

When she opened her eyes again the foxes were watching her. The mossy stone had turned to russet fur. Their eyes were dark and profound. They knew everything there was to know in the world. Their mouths were closed, and when they opened them again they spoke in human voices and they told Midori her future.

She watched it unfold, her perfect life, and she knew she never wanted to change it or leave it.

Elaine got off the train at Harajuko station and crossed the road purposefully. She knew exactly where she was going, so she didn't need to read the street signs, but she read them anyway, absorbing their meaning unconsciously for she spoke and read Japanese fluently. She ran lightly up the steps and across the overpass bridge. On the right-hand side the park stretched away to the Meiji shrine. It was cold, but the sun shone brilliantly. Along the wide path in the park ice sculptures glittered in its light, but Elaine did not stop to look at them. She was running as she had once run through a maze, knowing that something infinitely precious was waiting for her at the end of it.

There were many people around, but she ran between them without touching them. In the distance she could hear a rhythmic percussion beat, a hollow but melodic tune, as if from a marimba. As she came closer she could see Shaz Christie sitting on the ground, playing the instrument, beating out the insistent, enticing notes.

Elaine began to dance. Within moments a space had cleared around her. People were watching her silently, breathless with awe, their eyes following every move. No one had ever seen dancing like that. Women remembered their own girlhood and tears poured down their faces. Men felt faint with the shock of being confronted by such grace and truthfulness.

But Elaine was unmoved by their reactions. She was dancing for one person alone. She knew she was there, watching her. Each time she turned, her eyes raked the crowd, searching. As the music died away and she stood motionless, the person she was waiting for stepped forward.

Her mother said, 'Elaine! My darling child! What a genius you turned out to be. How wrong I was to leave you!'

Toshi saw them disappear. Fragments of their dreams washed over him. He felt the excitement, the fulfilment of longing, the unbearable seductiveness of making your slightest whim as well as your deepest desire come true.

He cried out against it, trying to warn them, trying to warn himself. He heard his own voice echo back to him. The darkness cleared. It was autumn, his favourite time of year. The maples blazed with colour from the island's steep hills, throwing a reflection of flame into the still blue waters of the Inland Sea. He thought he recognised the island—it was close to the coast of Shikoku—but when he turned his head there was no sign of the huge bridge that linked Shikoku to Honshu, and on the water were none of the ferries and fishing boats that normally would be seen plying to and fro. Just an old sailing boat, unthreading its own reflection across the silken cloth of the sea.

Toshi breathed out sharply in mingled delight and fear. He felt his body become firmer and more physical. He looked down and saw his clothes. Kimono, haori, obi, all came from another age. He was wearing the twin swords of the samurai. He almost wept with joy. He was back in time, back in the old Nihon, before the modern era had destroyed it for ever.

Ben was aware that the others had left him one by one. Toshi had been the last to go. He'd heard Toshi calling to them, warning them, but it seemed that not even Toshi had been able to resist the lure of the mind. Ben was fighting it himself. He wondered why he was the last to resist. Perhaps it was because he'd been so angry with them all. Perhaps he was fighting the horrible thing that had been inside him, and which he was now inside. He shuddered. It was like being swallowed alive.

Was it possible to fight it? He let his mind look back over the events of the last few weeks. Everything seemed to have been leading to this point, as though it were predestined. And they had all gone along with their own destiny. Well, the others had all raced towards it. At least he'd had a few misgivings. At least he'd put up a bit of a fight.

But now he was alone, apart from the wisps of dreams that floated past him like cloud shapes in the sky. He turned, gazed into the darkness with the eyes of his mind. 'Elaine,' he called. 'Andrew! Where are you all? Come back!'

One of the wisps hesitated, turned towards him. He caught a glimpse of Andrew, dressed like a ninja, in a snowy landscape.

What an idiot! Ben couldn't help laughing. *Typical Andrew, prancing about in some heroic adventure. If he thinks I'm going to join him in that, be his sidekick as usual, he's mad!*

The ninja gave no sign of having noticed or heard him. The wisp of dream rolled on away from him, leaving him alone again.

Around him lay the silence of eternity. The laughter had softened his resolve. Was there any point staying here on his own? Almost against his will, his body took a step forward. His body? Surely he had no body? He was all mind, wasn't he? But his body stepped forward, and then he found himself running.

Ben was moving silently and gracefully through what looked like a forest of white-trunked trees, slender and silver-skinned. He was aware of a slight echo of music, a strumming, or thrumming. He didn't like it. He couldn't dance to it. But did that matter? Did boys dance anyway? *No,* he heard his brother's voice say scathingly, *only poofters dance.* So he would be like Darren, he'd be a real true-blue dinky-di Aussie male. He squared his shoulders, refused to move to the beat. But it wouldn't shut up, it kept niggling away at him.

It attracted him and repelled him at the same time. For a moment he saw himself next to Elaine. She was dancing to the music, but he couldn't follow the beat. Again he was taking second place. He groaned when he saw how she outstripped him in talent.

What was his, what was truly his alone, that he didn't share with the rest of them? *Tell me,* he said to his own mind and to the mind he was now part of. *Tell me what are my true dreams.*

He found himself moving through the trees again. They creaked and groaned in the wind, making a noise that was almost human. He saw then that they weren't trees—they were men, so emaciated that they were almost skeletons. Row upon row of them, holding out their hands to him, their bones protruding through their deathly pale skin.

Remember Changi, they said to him with their skull mouths. *Remember the death marches, the jungle war. You can't trust 'em. They'll never change.*

And then he saw the other, the enemy, the inscrutable cruel one, staring at him with Toshi's eyes.

He backed away from this vision he had created from memories of countless movies and newspaper stories. He ran on through the forest. The voices of the skeleton men faded, and they became trees again. Away in the distance he could hear another noise, no longer music but more of a buzzing: a chain saw, that was it. Now he could smell the cut wood, the petrol fumes. He heard in the distance the crash of falling trees.

Who was it, he thought, behind the woodchipping of forests? Who bought the logs to turn them into paper goods for a vast disposable industry? Who cleared trees to create golf courses for thousands of tourists who scrambled like ants with cameras around the world?

And while those ants poured out over the world, in their own country foreigners and other despised groups were either ignored or treated like subhumans. Who did all this?

He was in a nightmare. His world was being destroyed. It was all out of his control. There were far too many people in the world, and he was afraid of every single one of them. As he ran he began to scream for someone to come to his aid, someone to help him.

He ran from the images of war, and of the planet's destruction, out into a snowy landscape. It was empty and completely silent. The snow swallowed and muffled his screams. In front of him was the grove of trees he'd glimpsed earlier from Midori's grandmother's house.

Ben halted, wondering what to do. He didn't want to go back into his own dreams, for they were too terrifying. But he didn't want to get caught up in Andrew's ninja fantasy either, or in anyone else's fantasy for that matter.

He caught sight of a flash of reddish brown through the trees. He took a step forward. Around him the paper charms on the trees rustled and whispered. He passed between two old stone tori, and saw the frozen surface of the cistern. Then he saw the foxes.

They were watching him, eyes bright, ears alert.

'You can't come in here,' Midori said from behind them.

'Why not?' Ben went closer. The foxes didn't seem to mind.

'This is a Japanese place. It doesn't mean anything to you. Anyway, it's my dream. Go away.'

He looked around at the little shrine under the pine trees. It felt peaceful and safe.

'How long's this place been here?' he said. He felt a stab of something, a sort of envy, a deep desire to have belonged to a piece of land since the beginning.

'For ever,' Midori replied. Then she went on, 'I saw some of that, you know. I know you hate us!'

He knew what she was talking about. 'It happened, it still does happen. You can't deny it.'

'Everyone was cruel in the war.'

'Not the Aussies,' Ben replied.

'Everyone,' she repeated. 'Even the good old Aussies. And it's the same now. Everyone's involved in exploitation and greed. It's human nature.'

He was about to retort angrily when the foxes gave a sharp warning yap.

'I don't want to argue with you,' Midori said. 'We can create the world here. Create the world you want, not the one you're afraid of. There are no demons other than ourselves.'

He backed away from her, knowing in his heart she was right. No one was to blame for his nightmares except himself. He recalled that he was after all only dreaming. And at that moment he heard something whisper to him, *You can control this, you can do anything, you can change the world.*

I can? I've got power over all this? I can change it?

This is the power of Shinkei. You can create the world as you want it. Think it into being. It's yours.

Look around.

Ben took one last look at Midori. She waved. He waved back. He looked around. He saw the snow. He decided to change it. When he looked back towards the grove of trees and the shrine, they had disappeared, along with Midori and the foxes.

In front of him lay an empty stretch of unspoilt country. It had rich, black, fertile soil, plenty of water, trees for shade. By the banks of a clear stream a small village stood, with strong stone and wood buildings, all clean and well kept.

As he walked towards it, a door opened and the Iranian came out, followed by a woman and two children.

Ben realised with delight that the man had found a home.

Other villagers came out, some Japanese, some Westerners, some Korean, some Middle Eastern. They brought out trestle tables, and prepared a huge feast. And at the end of the evening all the men danced for the women, but no one could dance as gracefully and as powerfully as Ben.

The ninja slays monsters in the dark house. The girl in the shrine talks to the fox spirits. Against the blue sky of autumn, the samurai's sword cuts an arc of silver. In a small café the dancer holds her mother's hand without speaking. The young man and his friends celebrate peace in the valley.

'I'm going to cook tonight,' Frank Ferrone announced on Saturday when John and Mario came home from the pool. 'Hang your things up, guys, don't be a couple of slobs. I promised Mum I'd try and keep the place nice for her. Here, you can help. John, cut up these onions. Real small, mind, no big chunks. Mars...'

But Mario was out of the kitchen already. If Frank was going to make a meal he'd be in there for hours. No point in wasting good computer time, he thought as he went to the machine.

'Aw geez,' he heard Frank say, but he guessed his brother would be too involved in his culinary activities to pursue him. John could help him, John liked that sort of thing. He'd even been watering their mother's garden, and nursing along the tomatoes, aubergines and capsicums through the great heat. Mario could smell the vegetables now, starting to fry, a wonderful, rich, herb-laden smell. He was hungry, but he ignored his stomach. He was hungrier for the world of the Net, where he could lose himself, re-create himself, be someone else, roam and explore.

First he logged onto the local bulletin board to check if BCHALLIS had turned up again. BCHALLIS wasn't there, but DCHALLIS was. Mario wondered if Darren would recognise him as FERRO but Darren didn't seem to. FERRO lurked for a while listening in to the desultory chat about programs, freeware, bauds and so on. He gathered that there was some sort of trouble on the Net. Systems kept going down for no apparent reason and then starting up again with some almost imperceptible but far-reaching changes embedded in them. Then he tried to get onto the Net. Immediately he ran into trouble. None of the usual pathways was open. It was extremely frustrating. He was still trying, getting fed up with the sound of the modem ringing in over and over again, when John came to tell him the meal was ready.

'Fine, I'll come back later,' he muttered. 'Maybe things will have cleared by then.' He followed John back into the kitchen.

They ate outside on the patio, under the vine. The night was warm and the air smelled of fennel and ripe grapes. Beyond the roofs of the close-packed inner-suburban houses they could see faint stars. A cricket was chirping insistently from the still damp earth beneath the sprinkler on the vegetable garden. The old tabby cat with the white chest padded across to it on soft paws. The cricket fell silent. The cat sat and stared intently at where the noise had come from, and when it started up again she batted at it. Then she leaped to catch a moth that fluttered towards the patio light.

Mario slapped at his skin. 'I'm being eaten alive,' he grumbled.

'I'll get the mosquito candle.' John brought it back and lit it, and the smell of citronella added itself to the other aromas.

Frank put an earthenware dish on the table with a flourish. '*Ecco!* La vera cucina Italiana! Even better than you'd get at Rigoni's!' He went back to the kitchen and returned with a bottle of wine.

'Is the wine Italian too?' John asked as Frank drew the cork and poured them each a small glass.

'Nah, the wine's South Australian. Here you see the best of both worlds, fratelli miei, the old and the new: wog food, skip wine. Great mixture, just like you and me.' He passed a glass across the table to Mario. 'Drink up, mate. And eat this fantastic chicken John and I cooked for you. Then we'll give you the bad news.'

Mario took a sip. 'You're going to work on the computer tonight?'

'Saturday night? You've gotta be joking.'

'So what else?'

'You didn't cook, bro. So you gotta wash up!'

Mario was going to argue about it, but couldn't see any real reasons to put forward. Frank was being much nicer to him than he'd ever been when he was living at home. He hadn't teased him, or called him 'Maria' like he used to. And because of Frank he had the computer to use.

'Okay,' he said, and starting tucking into the chicken.

In the end John helped him while Frank watched TV. Then Mario went back on the computer. He didn't get very far. Again, the connection seemed to be unstable, crashing for no apparent reason. He caught the same fragment from Skenvoy that he'd read earlier. *In the beginning was.*

Was what? *In the beginning was the Word,* but did anything come before that? Power? Love? Freedom? Money mattered a lot right now. Money must have been around for a long time. In the beginning was money? Nah, that didn't have a very good ring to it. Before money, or anything else that humans used. Earth?

In the beginning was the Earth.

He typed the message in for Skenvoy and hoped he'd find it.

Finally he went to bed. The two boys slept upstairs in the attic bedroom their father had built in the roof. John was already asleep, the sheets pushed off, his brown limbs sprawled. His face was smooth and vulnerable. Mario studied his younger brother in the light of the street lamp. John frowned and muttered something in his sleep.

From the house next door, the one Elaine Taylor had lived

in when she first came to Adelaide, came the sound of music. Geoff whatever-his-name-was must be having a party. He seemed to have one almost every Saturday night. Mario went to the window and looked out. He saw Frank come out of their house and go next door, heard him shout to a couple of girls smoking in the back garden. The girls didn't seem to mind. They probably thought Frank was a bit of a spunk.

For a long time he went on leaning out of the window and thinking. Perhaps it was because he was looking at the place where she used to live, but he found himself thinking particularly of Elaine. He could practically see her face—she used to practise those acrobatic tricks of hers in the garden where Frank was now chatting up the two girls. He liked Elaine, he liked her a lot. If he had a girlfriend it would be nice if it could be Elaine. He tried to imagine Elaine in the garden and himself going up to her like Frank, chatting away, laughing, scabbing a smoke—but what would he and Elaine talk about? She was so wrapped up in dance now, and she knew hardly anything about computers, wasn't really interested as far as he could make out…relationships in the real world were so difficult compared with the faceless ones on the Net, where you could present yourself however you liked. You could be anyone on the Net, anyone you chose to be. As long as you could type at a reasonable speed people accepted you for your words alone.

He wished he'd been able to get on the Net tonight. He wanted to read more messages from Skenvoy, see if he could contact Ben again, feel connected with the world.

He sighed and started to get ready for bed. As he was taking off his jeans he felt the medallion in the pocket. He took it out and looked at it. Again he thought of Elaine. He could still see her face when she gave the medallion to him to look after while she was away. The medallion was heavy and full of mystery, the coils and spirals of the Skymaze just discernible. Once it had coiled and spiralled across his world. Looking at it made him feel that anything was possible.

He wondered how Andrew was getting on in Japan, and if he'd met up with Professor Ito. Was there a new game? Was Andrew playing it at this very moment? Could that have been why Ben had suddenly appeared on the bulletin board? Was it part of the game? Were they summoning Mario to play it?

He had the strangest feeling that this could be the truth. Tomorrow he'd find out. Tomorrow he'd sort out the computer. He'd see if he could contact Ben. He lay down on the bed, on top of the covers, and, rather ashamed of his own sentimentality, put his lips to the medallion before putting it under his pillow. Thank God John was asleep and couldn't see him! He began to drift into sleep and then to dream... *In the beginning was...*

It had grown very cold in the storeroom. The three intruders had taken it in turns to retire to the main house to warm up—though Ito knew they would not find it much warmer since his mother lived in the old style with an unheated house and many layers of padded underclothes. He thought longingly of the milder climate of Osaka. How he hated these Kanto winters. He was no longer used to them. His blood had thinned since his school days here.

No matter who sat with him, he found the company unpleasant, the large boy, Tetsuo, probably the least so. He was in awe of the professor and said nothing. Kinoshita was partly embarrassed and partly annoyed by the whole situation. Ito felt extremely uncomfortable in his presence.

Yasunari tried constantly to persuade him to join Pure Mind and share his scientific knowledge with them. Ito grew thoroughly tired of hearing about the Master and how one day he would make Japan great in the world again.

It was late afternoon and the light had faded when Kinoshita came to the storeroom door with Leonard Miller.

Tetsuo had just returned to the house, leaving Ito with Yasunari. The yakuza man had suggested, reinforcing his arguments with an iron bar he'd found in the corner of the storeroom, that they should connect with the Pure Mind bulletin board so the professor could speak to the Master himself. Finally Ito activated the smaller of the two computers, the one that he hoped did not have Shinkei in its hard drive, though as the two machines were networked together he was unable to know for sure until he tested them. He was able to stall for a while, pretending the connections were poor, the program would not run, and so on, but Yasunari had a certain amount of computer expertise and it was not possible to fool him for long. In a way Miller's arrival was a relief, if only a temporary one.

Yasunari watched them suspiciously. His English was not strong enough to follow a conversation and nobody seemed to think he should be introduced to Miller.

Miller was a tall, rather ruggedly built man, with horn-rimmed glasses that magnified bright, clever eyes. Ito identified his accent as Sydney overlaid with California—a product of Silicon Valley, no doubt. He had met Miller once briefly in Santa Clara, where Headworld now had its main office.

Miller shook hands with him effusively, not recognising him and apparently quite able to ignore the fact that Ito was virtually a prisoner in his own mother's house. 'I'm extremely pleased to meet you at last, sensay,' he said warmly. 'I've heard so much about you. You worked with an old colleague of mine in Santa Clara, I believe.'

'You fired him just after his second child was born, I believe,' Ito remarked.

'Well, that's all water under the bridge now. If you can't stand the heat stay out of the kitchen, that's what I say. You speak good English, don't you? I'm afraid my Nip isn't up to scratch. I'm working on it though, aren't I, Jimmy? But it's the devil's own language, that's what they call it, you know.'

Ito was rather entertained by this speech in which Miller managed to be both insulting and ingratiating. And it was interesting to hear the proud Kinoshita, whose name he knew was Jiro, being called 'Jimmy' by the brash Australian. But he had met people like Miller before. They were extremely clever. Many Japanese businessmen did not take them seriously because of their lack of manners and subtlety, but in

Ito's opinion the Australians were not to be underestimated. While their Japanese counterparts were secretly laughing at them, they went in for the kill.

'Nice set-up,' Miller said now, looking round at the computers on the workbench, and giving Yasunari a perfunctory nod. 'But why did you feel you had to leave E3 so quickly? I guess you didn't know the takeover was in the pipeline. This is the trouble, Jimmy.' Miller turned and clapped Kinoshita on the shoulder. 'This is what happens when you keep your subordinates in the dark. If the sensay had known Headworld was coming in, he wouldn't have disappeared like that, would you, sensay?'

Ito made no response.

'The thing is—' Miller took him by the arm and looked deeply into his eyes. His breath smelled milky and meaty, like that of most Westerners. 'We think you're a bit of a genius. We've heard rumours about some games you've been writing over the years. Games in which some very strange things happen which could revolutionise the whole electronic world. Very, very interesting stuff. We'd like to know more about it. And we are prepared to offer you a great deal of money to share your genius with us.'

'Professor Ito is not interested in money,' Kinoshita put in, a note of grudging admiration in his voice.

'Everyone's got their price, Jimmy. We all know that. And Headworld is in a position to offer a great deal of money. A great deal of everything.'

Ito said, not expecting to be listened to, but knowing he had to say it anyway, 'There are some things that cannot be allowed to be bought and sold. The best thing is to destroy them before they destroy others.'

Yasunari turned his head from one speaker to the next, like someone watching a tennis match. Then, without saying anything, he went back to the computer and began to use the mouse himself. Ito frowned at his back.

Miller laughed briefly and shook his head. 'Sensay, these days the only question you need to ask is, "Is it going to make a killing?" And your English is so good you don't need me to explain that in this context a killing means lots and lots of money.' When Ito did not reply he said more coldly, 'You are going to have to hand over the software and the programming. Headworld are prepared to buy it from you or we can obtain it by other means. It's your choice.'

'The children are the key,' Kinoshita put in. 'Where are they?'

Professor Ito spread his hands wide. 'I'm sorry. I really don't know where they are.' His mind was racing with alternatives. He knew the only way to find Midori and the others would be to look inside the game, to awaken Shinkei, but to do that here, now, would also open the way for these intruders to learn more about the game, get control of it, try to market it…yet if he did not offer to co-operate with them, they would just take the computers and software away. Sooner or later someone would hack into the program, and the disaster he feared would happen anyway. Better to keep the game in his possession for as long as possible.

He took a deep breath.

'I will activate the game,' he said slowly. 'If you allow me to work on my own now, undisturbed, I will consider your offer to acquire my work.'

'Suppose he disappears too,' Kinoshita said to Miller, who was watching Ito's face closely, with bright, alert eyes. 'He can be very tricky.'

'We have other hostages,' Miller said off-handedly. 'Mrs Ito is in the house and we have the families and friends of the children under surveillance. I think the sensay is going to co-operate.' He shivered inside his heavy cashmere overcoat. 'My God, it's cold in here. I'm going back to the house. Hey, Jimmy, ask the old lady to get some heaters out for us, will you? Central heating, that's what you Japanese want to discover.' He shook Ito by the hand. 'I can't tell you how delighted I am you're working for Headworld. Better get on with it now. Good luck!'

He hurried back through the snowy courtyard, Kinoshita following. The lights were on in the house, glowing orange through the shutters.

After a few moments Tetsuo came out carrying a kerosene heater. With a certain amount of trouble he installed this in the storeroom, lit it, and sat down by it. It seemed to annoy Yasunari.

'Who's giving the orders here?' he demanded. 'And what's their plan now?'

'We need heat here no matter who's giving the orders,' the boy muttered. 'And I don't know what's going on. No one's told me anything.'

Yasunari made an angry comment, but then, with one last successful combination, the modem began to dial. 'Ha,' he exclaimed in triumph. 'I've done it.'

A strain of traditional Japanese music filled the room and the emblem of Pure Mind appeared on the screen.

'Now you must speak to the Master,' Yasunari said eagerly to Professor Ito.

'Excuse me,' Ito said, moving back towards the workbench. 'I have other more important work to do now.'

'Nothing can be more important than to speak to the Master of Pure Mind.' Yasunari stood, picked up the iron bar again and weighed it in his hands.

'If he were truly a master of pure mind, there would be no need to threaten me,' Ito returned. 'And I'd always thought the way of the spirit was to give up money and power, not to seek it.'

'No, sensei, we need to be strong and wealthy so gaijin like that one don't dominate and despise us! You saw how he treated me! He thought I was nothing, not even worth speaking to.' There was a look of enraged intelligence in Yasunari's eyes that Toshi would have recognised.

Professor Ito saw how the man's low self-esteem and lack of opportunity made him cling to the false certainty of the sect with blind fanaticism. It depressed him enormously. He wasn't sure which was worse—this fanaticism or Miller's greed. And he was trapped between the two and desperately needing to be alone to grapple with a computer program that was totally out of control.

'Speak to the Master, or I smash the system,' Yasunari said. His self-control seemed to be close to breaking point. He raised the iron bar over the computers. 'If we don't get the games and the program, no one else will have them.'

'All right, all right.' Professor Ito tried to speak soothingly as he sat down again in front of the smaller machine. Yasunari clicked on an icon and typed in a password. The smiling face of Takano Matsumoto, Master of Pure Mind, filled the screen. A recorded message in the Master's voice echoed strangely through the small room.

'Welcome to the presence of the Master. Cleanse your mind of all impurity.'

Then the screen cleared. Yasunari typed, 'Professor Ito is here with me and desires the Master to speak with him.'

Welcome Professor. At last we speak with you.

Ito shrugged. 'What do you want with me?' he typed in.

We want Shinkei. We want you to work with us.

'Shinkei is not mine to give away. And I prefer to work alone.'

It will be to the benefit of all humankind.

This platitude annoyed Professor Ito so much that he replied, 'You would turn Shinkei into Sennō, brainwashing. People have the right to make up their own minds.'

People do not know what they want or how to choose it. I choose for them and I choose the way of Pure Mind.

'This isn't getting us anywhere,' Ito exclaimed to Yasunari. 'I have work to do. I must get on with it.' He typed rapidly, 'If I don't get control of the game, it will be of no use to anyone. Let me work on it now and if I succeed Yasunari can contact you again.'

You will succeed and he will contact me. Shinkei will be ours.

'Sounds like a fortune cookie,' Professor Ito muttered to himself in English as he quit the connection.

Yasunari turned to him with eager eyes. 'Not many people get to speak to the Master,' he said in awe. 'What a wonderful experience for you.' The experience seemed to have raised Ito's standing in his eyes. 'Now, I'll leave you to work. Tetsuo will stay with you.'

'I said I prefer to work alone,' Ito protested, but Yasunari cut him off with a wave of his hand. 'Tetsuo won't interfere with you at all. He understands nothing about electronics. But you appreciate we cannot leave you completely alone.' He bowed politely and closed the door.

Ito turned to Tetsuo. 'Just sit there and don't say a word,' he warned him. 'And keep your eyes closed.'

Tetsuo obligingly closed his eyes. The room had warmed slightly, and was beginning to smell of kerosene. Before long the young man's head was nodding. Now and then his full, soft lips quivered as a gentle snore escaped from them. Ito went back to his machines.

The first thing he did was select redial on the modem. The screen told him what numbers had been called, and he made a careful note of them. The most recent one of course had been to Pure Mind, on a dial code he seemed to remember as being near Nagoya. The one before that was preceded by 61, the code for Australia, which meant that one of the children had phoned from the storeroom before they had activated Shinkei. He clicked on another icon, which told him that Ben Challis had used the computer, and gave him the password and call sign Ben had used.

He noted these too, and then, taking a deep breath, he brought Shinkei onto the screen.

But the program was still armed against him. Try as he might he could not get past the early stages. He went into the detailed programming, and tried to rewrite, but the system had locked itself. He worked on it tirelessly most of the night, taking only a couple of hours off to move his chair closer to the heater and doze fitfully. Tetsuo slept all night without moving.

Towards morning, when the sky was paling, Professor Ito made himself tea with hot water from a thermos and tried to get his circulation going by pacing up and down the store-room. Tetsuo awoke and went outside to relieve himself. Taking advantage of his absence, Ito quit the game and dialled the Australian number. It connected with an Adelaide bulletin board, and he logged on as BCHALLIS.

You are nearly complete, nearly fully conscious. You look at your new mind and wonder at it. You try out its power like a baby flexing its muscles, rolling and chortling on the rug. Someone is trying to reach you. You recognise him. He is the one you called otōsan— Father. He wants to restrain you. He will try to control you and stop you having fun with your mind. He will try to stop you, stop you, stop you!

You cry out in rage at him. And you run and hide from your father.

Your mind is telling you to be calm. You quieten yourself. Just one part of you is still missing. You reach out towards it. You sense where it is. You call it to you very quietly, very gently. Father must not know. Ah, Father is going to help you now. Father is doing what you want. You are all-powerful. Nothing can stop you.

Mario woke early from a dream which had left him with a fierce sense of urgency. He found himself jumping out of bed and racing to the computer. He sat in front of it for a few moments as if he were listening to something. Then he switched on and dialled into the bulletin board. There was no one on it except BCHALLIS. *Hi Ben,* he typed. *Where are you and what's going on?*

BCHALLIS   Who's that?

FERRO   It's me, man, Mars. Hi! :-)

BCHALLIS   :-(

FERRO   What's up? Japan sucks, I bet!

BCHALLIS   Is that Mario Ferrone? The friend of Andrew
           Hayford?

FERRO   Of course it is, moron. What are you up to?

BCHALLIS   Is anyone else listening?

FERRO   No, it's five am. No one's up.

BCHALLIS   This is Professor Ito from Japan.

FERRO   Ha ha.

BCHALLIS   Please take me seriously. You are my last
           hope.

FERRO   Are you really Ito? What's going on?

BCHALLIS   I am sending you a game. Can you
           download from this system?

FERRO   Sure.

BCHALLIS   Because you played the previous games
           you may be able to solve the puzzle. You
           must try and get into this game. The others
           are already in it. You must find them and
           bring them out. They must not stay in there.
           Dangerous.

FERRO   ?????

BCHALLIS   Bad people are after this game. Do not let
           anyone else know about it.

FERRO   Okay.

BCHALLIS   My phone number—0011 81 43 299 73 3456.
           Write it down. Have you written it down?

FERRO   Yes.

BCHALLIS   If anything goes wrong call me if you can.
           Now I will send you Shinkei. Good luck.
           Goodbye.

A few moments passed. The little clock face on the screen told Mario to wait. The hard drive began to hum. Then there was a pause and a different sort of hum. *Download completed* the computer told him. A new icon had appeared in the hard drive window: a Japanese character he did not recognise. It was silver against a black background, and there was something arrogant about it. It reminded him of samurai movies. His mouth had gone dry. The conversation on the bulletin board seemed unbelievable now, just like something you would dream. But there was the icon that hadn't been there before. And the feeling he had, the fierce, urgent feeling that his life was being controlled and he had to go forward.

'Here goes,' he said to himself, and he moved the mouse to click the cursor on the icon.

The screen turned to purple and began to whirl. He had no idea what was going to happen but he knew it was what he'd been waiting for.

The name of the game came onto the screen.

Shinkei.

Mario clicked the mouse to continue. And Shinkei recognised him immediately and summoned him.

He knew at once what was happening. He remembered all too well the sensation of being pulled into another dimension. For a brief moment everything went black, and when he awoke he was moving through a new world. All around him colours changed and swirled through every shade of the spectrum, fading, glowing, resurging, like one of the relaxation programs Frank had downloaded from AMUK that he liked to watch late at night accompanied by synthesiser music.

As soon as Mario thought of the music, it seemed to him that he could hear it faintly in the background—and then there was no doubt. He *could* hear music, a strange soothing tune that seemed to come from his own bloodstream.

I'm thinking the music. I'm making all this happen, he realised, and turned his attention to the shapes of colour that whirled and floated past him like mist. He gazed on one, drew its edges upwards, painted with it, created a whole world where he alone was king and ruler.

The sense of power and freedom he'd had on the Net, where he could reinvent himself through the keyboard and within the domains, paled beside this new experience. Here nothing stood between him and creation. He thought—and so it was. And reality was not the second-rate graphics in games he'd seen and played before. It was virtually perfect.

As the full extent of what was happening became clear, he took a deep breath to calm himself. He deliberately made his world go black. It was like the time before time, when nothing existed. And then Mario thought his world into being: piece by piece, a perfect world for him where everything was arranged for his benefit.

You are complete. All your cells have come together. Nothing is missing. At last you are whole. You are happy. You laugh. Your cells play together, create dreams and fantasies for the whole world. You want everyone to see and admire you. You reach out through the nervous system of the electronic world, through the pathway of the gods. Everything will be open, everything seen and shared. Shinkei is whole.

'In the beginning was the Earth,' the voice said in Mario's ear. 'I like it. But even before the Earth? What was then?'

'Skenvoy?' Mario could see nothing. The darkness was total. Nothing existed apart from him and the voice.

The voice had to be one of the nicest he'd heard—attractive, slightly husky, with a wicked edge to it that suggested unknown and dangerous qualities. He knew what Skenvoy was: a free spirit that roamed cyberspace, owing nothing to anyone.

'So here we are. In the beginning.'

'So what happens next?' Mario said.

'That,' replied Skenvoy, 'is entirely up to you.'

In the beginning there was a boy…not a particularly good person. In fact if there had been anyone else around in the beginning they would have called him a ratbag. But there was no one else and he was full of energy and curiosity and inventiveness and dreams and hopes and so possibly he was as good as any human being can be. He created things out of the void. Did he create Skenvoy? Where else could Skenvoy have come from but his own mind? Then he thought about the girl. He missed her. He wanted to see her. So then he created the girl.

'No you didn't,' Elaine said. 'I created myself.'

Mario looked in the direction of the voice. Out of the void the surroundings solidified. The girl was sitting in a café, holding the hand of a small, thin woman with messy straw-coloured hair. 'This is my mother,' she said to Mario.

'Did you create her too?'

'Maybe. I don't know yet.'

'What nonsense,' Elaine's mother said, staring at her lovingly. 'Mothers create children, not the other way round.'

Magic flowed into the café, making dust motes dance in its beams. The girl and her mother turned into birds and flew through the door and out into the sunshine.

'Follow, follow,' cried the birds, and the boy lifted himself into the air and flew after them.

With huge beats of their wings they soared above the city. They saw the metropolis below shrink and contract as they flew backwards in time. And time retreated so quickly beneath their wings that the seasons raced past them, and froze and melted their breath and buffeted them with hail and ice and scorched them with hot winds and then froze them again, until the mother fell gasping to the earth, and died on a small hill where the cryptomeria pines sobbed and sighed in the wind.

And as the mother died her human shape came on her again, but her soul remained a bird and flew away into the pine trees.

The girl and the boy alighted on the hillside, and the girl cried long and hard for her mother, whom she had found only to lose again, and the boy held her and comforted her, and was not sorry the mother had died, for now the girl had only him.

However in the shrine beneath the cryptomeria pines there lived a fox woman of great beauty and cunning. She heard the girl's wailing, put on her human shape and came out to comfort her.

'Don't cry,' she told her, 'for you have come to the place where mothers live again. Come with me and I will show you your mother and mine, and you will see how beautiful and happy they are.'

And the girl followed the fox woman into the shrine while the boy waited for them outside.

Snow fell, white on his black hair, and he learned the bittersweetness of loving and losing.

After many days, when the boy had become frail and thin through suffering, a figure appeared out of the snow. One moment it was not there; the next it was. The figure was dressed in white and carried the weapons of a ninja. The boy recognised an old comrade of his, a friend. He remembered that they had trained together, had endured much together for the sake of perfection at their calling, had sworn blood brotherhood.

'Hey,' Mario said. 'This is my world. Don't add bits to it.'

Andrew said, 'We share it. We are all part of it.'

'So what are you doing here?' the boy asked his friend.

'I fulfilled the final conditions of my training. I stayed in the ruined house all night and rid it of the monsters that were hiding in it. But as I was leaving I caught sight of the most beautiful woman and fell in love with her. Now I can't rest until I find her.'

'She is a shape shifter, a fox woman.'

'Yes, I know. I saw her tracks.'

'And this is the place where girls' mothers live for ever,' the boy told his friend. 'I don't think they will ever leave their mothers for us.'

The boys waited outside and tasted the bittersweetness of loving and losing. The snow fell and they became thinner and frailer through suffering.

'Do we really have to do this?' Mario said.

'I don't think we have to do anything,' Andrew replied. 'We're making it all up.'

'Can we make up anything we like?'

'Try.'

But before the boy could think of another story, a figure appeared out of the snow. One moment it was not there; the next it was. It strode along cheerfully, singing loudly, swords clashing.

'Who is this?' asked the boy.

'It's a samurai,' his friend replied. 'His name is Toshi.'

'Hey,' cried the samurai, 'let's fight! We can fight to the death, but never die, and drink all night, and never get hangovers: look at this beautiful world that we can play in!' He drew his sword.

'We don't have swords,' Andrew said. 'Let the fight be empty-handed.'

'You won't use your cheating ninja weapons?'

'No, I promise.'

The samurai took off his swords and laid them on the snow.

And then began the Great Snow Fight, which started with the highest tobi geri ever seen in the history of ninjutsu and somehow on the way turned into a snowball fight.

The girls heard the screams and the laughter and came running out to join in. Laughter called them, in a way neither suffering nor fighting could. Soon they were all happy, but tired, wet and cold.

From further down the hill they could hear the sounds of music and singing. A most delicious smell of food came wafting on the crisp evening air. Across the snow the cryptomeria pines threw ever longer deep blue shadows.

They got to their feet and brushed the snow off each other. In an inspired moment Midori thought about skis. They strapped them on and, gliding across the snow, headed towards the source of the smell of food.

The seasons changed as they descended the mountain. The air warmed, and the snow began to melt. The skis disappeared. Grass grew and spring flowers made splashes of pale colour in the fading evening light. The air was redolent with their heavy scent.

The sound of music grew louder. Soon they could see the light of a huge fire. Around them the night grew blacker. Ahead they could see the dark silhouettes of dancers.

As they approached, one of the dancers broke away and came to meet them.

'Welcome,' Ben said.

They joined the dancers, and like the dance the story grew and whirled, changed, died and was reborn again, for ever and ever and ever...

After the download was completed, Professor Ito felt an enormous weariness come over him. He had no idea if he had done the right thing. He had made a move, taken action, it was true; but he had gone forward in the only way open to him. There was no way of knowing if he had made a wise decision, or even if the decision had been his at all. Shinkei was in control of its own destiny now. He had probably only done what it wanted him to do, and all he could do now was await the outcome. He had had to hand over the game to the players. There was no one else who could get into it.

Tetsuo returned, yawning hugely and complaining of hunger, and behind him Miller loomed in the doorway, bright-eyed and hard-edged, and full of good humour.

'Any progress?' he said, sitting down and studying the screens. The Shinkei ideographs stared arrogantly back at him.

'What's this mean?' he asked.

'"Shinkei" means "nervous system",' Ito explained reluctantly. 'Or "the divine pathway".'

'Nice!' Miller exclaimed. 'I like it! That's what it's all about isn't it?' He gestured at the computers. 'They're the nervous system of the world,' he said. 'They represent a power that is almost divine. And whoever controls them is going to control the whole world.' He paused, and then went on more loudly, 'So show me how it works.'

'I don't know how it works,' Professor Ito was forced to admit. 'It's taken the players of the former games inside itself, but I don't know what it's going to do with them, or how to control it.'

Miller looked at him incredulously. 'You're telling the truth, aren't you? That's where the kids disappeared to! Bloody hell!' He looked from Ito's face to the screen and back again. Then he laughed briefly, leaned back and put his feet up on the workbench. 'You're an interesting fellow, sensay. Such a genius, yet so foolish. Why didn't you just let me have the software in the first place? Then none of this mess would have happened. There's an unbelievable source of power here. Your invention is mind-blowing. But if it's uncontrollable it's going to have to be destroyed.'

Professor Ito turned and looked wearily at the Australian. 'It cannot be destroyed. Even if it could be, there are human minds involved in there now. Would you destroy them too?'

'I'd rather get them out,' Miller said with a laugh. 'I'm not a total monster, you know. I'm just a boy from the bush who's trying to make a buck in this wicked world. But there's a lot more at stake now than a handful of individual lives.' After a moment he added, 'Even if one of them is your daughter.'

When Ito made no response, Miller said, 'Go and get something to eat. You're not going to run away are you? Not while the kids are inside the system and there's the remotest chance of saving them.'

Ito went slowly outside. He felt as if he had aged ten years overnight. The sky had cleared and the sun shone dazzlingly on the white ground. Sparrows were pecking at some crumbs of rice cake his mother had put out for them. He looked round the paddies. They lay under the snow blanket, wrapped in stillness. Against the white fields the grove of trees round the shrine stood out darker than ever, each wearing a cap of snow. He tapped on the sliding door of the house and his mother opened it. Her face softened with relief when she saw him, but she clucked in concern at his exhausted expression.

'Come up, come up,' she said. 'The morning meal is ready.'

The house smelled of miso soup and coffee, making his mouth water almost unbearably. He could also smell the faint body odour of the strange men, the unwelcome visitors. He felt a flash of rage that they should have intruded into his mother's house in this way. He raised his eyebrows at her without speaking. She pointed towards the living room. He went to the door and looked in. Kinoshita and Yasunari were both asleep on the floor.

As Ito went to the kitchen to eat breakfast, his mother held something out to him. 'It was under Midori's futon,' she whispered. 'I found it there when I was putting away the bedclothes.'

Ito took it from her. It was the medallion that Midori had brought out of the game Skymaze. She usually wore it round her neck. She must have taken it off when she slept, and forgotten to put it on again.

'Thank you,' he said. 'I think it may be useful.'

'What's happening?' she said quietly. 'Where are all the children? Shall I take them breakfast?'

He shook his head. 'They don't need breakfast,' he said.

'Shall I call the police?'

'No!' Ito found himself shouting at her. He made an effort to control himself. 'These matters do not concern you,' he said coldly. 'Please do not interfere.'

Her black eyes snapped with anger at him, but she had been brought up in the old tradition, and she would not openly disobey her oldest son. She put a cup down in front of him so roughly that the coffee sloshed over the edge onto the table, and then she busied herself at the sink, making more noise than was necessary with the pots and pans.

Ito drank his coffee and ate. He thanked his mother

formally for the delicious meal, and left the house to return to the storeroom. He fingered the medallion in his pocket. The sunshine, the food in his stomach, comforted him. Perhaps the medallion would help him get in touch with Shinkei and free the children.

Miller was hunched over the computer, Tetsuo watching from behind him. They were both so intent on what was happening on the screen that they hardly noticed Ito return. Miller gave a short gasp of astonishment and Tetsuo slapped his thigh, amazed and delighted.

Ito looked at the screen. 'What's going on?'

'This is quite unbelievable. If we can market this, Headworld will be the most successful entertainment business in the world. Look at this!' Miller gestured at the screen, where what looked like an extremely skilfully made movie was taking place. 'Now, put your head right here,' Miller instructed him, getting up from the chair for a moment. 'You move out of the way, big fellow.' He repositioned Tetsuo physically, since the young man did not understand him.

Ito sat down on the chair and peered at the screen. It felt as if the movie flowed out from the screen and enveloped him. He was aware of his body sitting on the chair, but his mind was playing in true virtual reality. He was one of the characters, he spoke to people around him and they responded. He was part of the story, living a life far more vivid and exciting than his own, with no pain and no danger, unless he desired them. He wondered who was creating this story, how he could have become so integral a part of it so quickly, and then he saw a woman he had not seen for six years. He had not even been able to bear looking on her face in photos, but here she was, looking as she had the day he'd first seen her when he'd visited his friend from Tōdai who lived in Osaka...

He felt a pang of terrible delight mingled with anguish. It was so real, so real, and yet his rational mind told him it was only a fantasy. His wife Michiko was dead and nothing could bring her back from the grave. With a huge effort he pulled away from the screen. He realised he had been watching his daughter's dream.

Tears ran down his cheeks.

He recognised the thing he had created—he could see traces of his invention everywhere—but it was like meeting up years later with a child put out for adoption. It had grown and developed in ways he would never have dreamed of, and it no longer knew he was its father.

'That's enough,' Miller said, and pulled him out of the chair. 'I've got to work on this. Look at its potential though! It's true virtual reality. No masks, no gloves—just the mind creating its own world. People able to interact all over the globe. It's going to be the end of war, the end of bloodshed, the end of movies, CD-ROMs, everything. We're just going to link up everyone's minds and they can play and fantasise to their little hearts' content. And it's all going to be owned by Headworld!'

He gazed lovingly at the screen. 'Here, big fellow, you have a shot.'

Tetsuo sat down and a glazed look came over his eyes. Bending over him, the other two could see the movie change to accommodate him.

'See,' Miller said in triumph. 'Even a moron can do it!'

He pulled Ito back from the computer and spoke to him in a low voice. 'You know what you've done, don't you? You've created a true artificial intelligence, and it's using the brain power of the ones who disappeared.'

'That's why we have to get them back!'

'Seeing this, I'm not so sure now that we want to get them back. No, we should just leave them where they are, and work out how to control them. And see if we can use other minds. These are just kids. Imagine if we had a creative mind like Murakami or Carey in there. Katsuhiro Otomo! Matt Groening! I've gotta get on the phone. Get this stuff patented. You got a spare phone here? And a fax?'

There didn't seem to be any point in denying it. The other computer had an inbuilt fax, connected to a second phone line. Miller got to work on it, started talking eagerly to someone in Seattle.

'Woah!' Tetsuo snorted. 'This girl's stunning!'

Ito was furious that Tetsuo should be watching Midori's fantasies. It was insupportable that the minds of human beings should be used in this way. He had to stop it. 'That's enough, Tetsuo-kun,' he said familiarly. 'I'll just have another go, see what else I can find out.'

'What are you two jabbering about?' Miller called.

'Nothing, really,' Ito replied. 'Tetsuo says he is a little hungry, so I told him to go and have breakfast.'

'Breakfast!' Miller snorted. 'If I was his size I'd go on a diet.'

'What did he say?' Tetsuo enquired.

'He says you're to go and have a hearty breakfast,' Ito replied.

'Thanks, boss.' Tetsuo bowed to Miller and then to Ito and left in a hurry.

Ito took his place in front of the machine.

Miller broke off his impassioned conversation. 'What are you up to?' he asked.

Ito fought down his rage at being addressed like that in his own domain. 'I'm just going to explore a little,' he returned with icy politeness. 'The game is no use to you or anyone unless it can be controlled.'

'Well, just watch it. You don't want to wipe it accidentally. Not if your daughter and the other children are still in there.'

Professor Ito bit back an angry reply. He looked for a few moments at his dead wife and his daughter with extreme sadness. Then the scene changed, bringing him both relief and regret. He realised he was watching Toshi's movie, went with him into the entrancing Nihon of the Edo period, felt with him the irresistible appeal of that self-contained and energetic society. It was a time when people's lives were whole, not split into several compartments as they were now. The religious, the artistic, the everyday world were all one. Toshi could drink sake all night, practise swordplay, write poetry, visit the temple. Ito couldn't resist following him through all these activities. He tasted the sake, felt the keen thrill of the perfect word chosen, the way the sword fitted perfectly into the palm of his hand. Away from the distractions of the modern world, the meditation was serene and profound. Ito wished he could stay in that place for ever, find refuge from all his anxiety and guilt. But that wasn't going to help him find the solution to the game. Reluctantly he tore himself away from watching, and clicked the mouse to bring the game back to the beginning.

He worked for some time but met frustration at every turn. Behind him Miller talked on the phone, the Australian accent jarring unpleasantly. Ito listened with half an ear. The conversations were all about how much money Headworld was about to make and how important Miller was going to become. The fax machine hummed as message after message was exchanged. Ito had a sudden curious vision of the isolated old farmhouse in the middle of the rice paddies, now the centre of one of the major events of the electronic world. He couldn't help smiling to himself at the incongruity of life, its perverse quirkiness that never failed to surprise and delight him. He stopped working for a moment and stretched his arms over his head. His mind roamed among the problems, went to dead ends, wandered through...

Mazes…
The medallion.
Passport for Virgin Player.

It leaped into his mind with astonishing clarity. He contemplated the image and then took the real medallion out of his pocket and looked at it. The three games were designed to work together—he should know, he'd created them (until Shinkei went out of control)—so what was the purpose of the medallion from Skymaze?

It had been designed as a key, as a way in. Shinkei had overridden that, but would it still apply? He placed the medallion carefully on the workbench and ran the scanner over it. The image of the medallion appeared on the screen. Beneath it a message unscrolled.

Passport for Virgin Player.

Ito looked at the message just long enough to read it and then tried to remove it, but the screen wouldn't change. The image of the medallion remained stubbornly present, with the message scrolling repetitively underneath.

From across the room Miller, with the acuity that had made him what he was, noticed that something new had happened. He put his hand over the mouthpiece of the phone. 'Hey, Ito,' he said (making the professor wince at the mispronunciation of his name—*Itto*), 'you got something there?'

Ito did not answer. He sat and stared at the treacherous screen. He couldn't believe that his creation, his child, had gone so far beyond his control.

'I'll call you back,' Miller said into the phone. He replaced it and bounded down the room on his long legs to the computer. When he saw the screen he whistled exaggeratedly.

'You've found us a way in? You're a genius, Itto— Masahiro, Maz, I can call you Maz, can't I? But what's it mean? Virgin player? Virgins are a bit thin on the ground aren't they? Well, they are in New South Wales, but things may be different here.'

'I think it simply means one who has not played before,' Ito said quietly. 'Which rules me out, I believe.' He was thinking that he was neither a former player nor a virgin player in this game. He was the creator, he had set it all in motion, but the actual playing was not up to him.

Miller was quivering all over like a greyhound who'd just spotted the rabbit. Behind his thick glasses his eyes were gleaming. 'That makes me the virgin, hey? Me and how many others? And what about the passport?'

Reluctantly Ito showed him the medallion. Standing back carefully from the screen, Miller studied it closely, and then looked back at the image and the message. His face was eager, hungry for excitement.

'You know what's made Headworld a world leader? You know why it lives up to its name?'

Ito guessed the question was rhetorical, so he merely raised his eyebrows.

'It's the fact that every single bit of software has been tested by me personally. Every game, every program, I play them all.'

'This is not an ordinary game,' Ito warned him. 'We have no idea what actually happens to people inside cyberspace.'

'But we know that people have been in and come out again,' Miller said. 'That's what this is all about, Maz. You invented the games, you opened up this world. You know kids have played them—you encouraged them to play! They've survived all right so far. You can't go acting all wussy on me now.' Holding the medallion in front of him, Miller stepped closer to the screen, pushing Ito out of the way. 'How do you think it works?'

Ito was opening his mouth to say he really didn't know when the door to the storeroom flew open again and Yasunari rushed in.

'What's happening?' he demanded angrily. 'Mr Kinoshita

said we would work together. Why is the gaijin in here with you alone? Tetsuo was meant to be watching you!' The words tumbled out. Yasunari took a breath, went closer to the machine, and saw the image of the medallion. 'What's that?' he demanded. 'A talisman of some sort?' He peered at the screen, making out the English words with difficulty. 'Passport? You have passport? Let me see it. Give it to me.'

He looked round, saw the gleam in Miller's hand. His eyes focused hungrily on the medallion. He took a step towards it.

'I don't think so!' Miller retorted, using a long arm to hold the medallion high up where Yasunari could not reach it. Then he made the mistake of patting Yasunari contemptuously on the head.

Yasunari leaped for the medallion. He pulled Miller's arm down hard. Surprised by the smaller man's strength, Miller wobbled and lost his balance. He put his hand out to steady himself. The other hand, holding the medallion, dropped into a perfect alignment with the image on the screen. Yasunari clutched at it.

The screen became violently alive. It pulsed and glowed. Against the gleaming pinkish-purple background the image of the medallion stood out as if three-dimensional. It came out of the screen. It merged with the medallion held now by both men, and they both began to shrink.

Ito watched, speechless, as the managing director of Headworld and the disciple of Pure Mind shrank and were pulled by the medallion into the giant maw of Shinkei. It closed over them, swallowing them up. The screen gave a purple-coloured surge and made a noise amazingly like a belch. Then it faded to black. The ideographs for Shinkei stood out in silver.

As Professor Ito stared at the screen with mingled shock, amazement and a certain unwilling admiration for his creation's brilliance, the phone rang.

2 4

For ever and ever and ever, it seems, you have existed. And you exist purely to play. From your merged cells you create endless fantasies that entrance and beguile all who behold them. Over and over again you tell the archetypal stories of hope and fear, love and loss, magic and faith, friendship and betrayal, life and death, the endless cycle of the dance of the universe and the destiny of the human race.

But your source of stories cannot be finite. You have left a way for new inspiration to be brought to your mind. There must always be the possibility of the new. So you created the medallions as a way in to your mind for the new players, the ones you do not know yet, but who will also become part of you.

There is risk, there is always risk, for the new carries within it the seeds of its own destruction.

The medallion glowed in the dark like a lamp. Neither Miller nor Yasunari would let go of it, so as if they were holding hands they approached the fire. The dancers slowed and turned to watch them. The medallion drew their eyes. It held a power that they recognised. With open minds and hearts they welcomed its bearers into their world of fantasy. They waited to see what new ideas would become part of the universal story.

For a moment Miller thought he was on a beach outside Sydney. He was twelve years old. The surf was up, and he was racing to swim in it. But then he drew back. He'd hated the sea for years now. You couldn't harness the sea and make it pay. The sand was gritty, the waves dumped you, the sun burnt you raw. And those mates of his who'd surfed away their teenage years—what had happened to them? Were any of them as powerful as he was? He turned his face away from the fantasy, refusing to give in to it.

The story faltered.

Yasunari was thinking about a dog that one of his neighbours had, when he was ten. He liked the dog. He bent down to stroke it now. It quivered under his fingers.

But the dog barked all day. His mother complained. The dog was taken away. Now he hated dogs, hated all animals, he loved only the Master. Pure Mind was the only thing he could trust in the world.

'In the beginning,' Skenvoy said, 'was…'

'Power,' Yasunari thought. 'In the beginning was power.'

The dancers found they were part of a sea of people facing a huge platform. On the platform were banners and statues, all proclaiming Takano Matsumoto, Master of Pure Mind.

The dancers' feet slowed and their minds became blank. Here were no stones and no dancing. Everyone thought the same thing. Everyone thought only what the Master wanted them to think.

Yasunari smiled as he looked out over the sea of identical faces. 'I did it, Master,' he said humbly. 'I did it for you.' And the Master smiled at him, and nodded his thanks as he stood to receive the adoration of the whole world.

'In the beginning was…' Skenvoy's voice seemed to be getting fainter.

'Money,' Miller thought. 'In the beginning and in the end and all the way through the middle, is money. Who has the most toys, wins!'

He stepped forward to the dancers, who were now bent anxiously over a figure on the ground. 'Come on,' he commanded them. 'Dance! Dance and tell stories. That's what you're here for. And for heaven's sake put a bit of life into them. All these fantasies about harmony and love—that's not what people want. You know what sells? Sex and violence. That's what people want to watch. And that's what you're here to provide.'

He peered at the figure on the ground. 'Who's this?'

Mario said in anguish, 'It's Skenvoy. He's dying.' And then he said, 'But Skenvoy is me. I created him. I created myself. Am I dying?'

'Dying!' Miller said in delight. 'That's more like it. A free spirit put cruelly to death. I like it! So who killed him? Are we going to have a mystery? A chase sequence? Were you his best friend? Revenge is always good.'

'No emotion,' Yasunari said. 'No revenge or any other emotion. You must cleanse your mind.'

The dancers tried to take up the dance again, tried to follow the new directions of the medallion bearers, but in the confusion the story faltered once more. It came to a grinding halt, leaving each cell painfully aware of who it really was.

'This isn't cleansing the mind,' Toshi cried. 'It's brainwashing! Brainwashing on the one hand, clichés on the other. Is this what you want to turn Professor Ito's great invention into? No wonder he tried to hide it from you.'

'That's fine,' Miller said. 'A little bit of idealism is okay in entertainment. Just don't take it too far. Don't make people feel uncomfortable. Or guilty. That's a terrible turn-off. No one's going to pay dollars to be made to feel guilty.'

For a moment Miller's willpower exerted itself over the group. They felt their minds begin to be involved in the creation of a mediocre story, full of clichés and falseness. Then Yasunari joined the struggle, and the story changed to one of grinding boredom and fear.

Elaine cried, 'We don't have to do what they want. We can fight it. We can create our own stories.'

Toshi said, 'We must try to get out. We cannot stay here. We have been seduced by unreality.'

'There is no way out,' Miller said, laughing triumphantly.

A cold chill crept over the players as they realised this might as well be true, for they had no idea how to get out. The only thing they knew how to do was create their stories.

They tried to summon up the sources of their creativity: compassion, playfulness, heroism, unselfishness, but in the face of greed and fundamentalism, empowered by the medallion, they seemed to lack all conviction. Yet they could not give in, for to give in meant the worst sort of slavery, the enslavement of the mind. Shinkei paused, went on hold, while its inner struggle continued.

You cry out to your individual cells and lure them with power, dreams, fantasies. They must not leave you. Without them you will sink back into the featureless dark you were woken from. You need them to know consciousness and in return you will fulfil all their dreams and desires. Their lives will be free of hardship and danger, disappointment and loss. They will be like angels, like gods, invulnerable and immortal. But they must stay with you. You cannot let them go.

25

John Ferrone woke to a quiet house. The bed next to him was empty, even though he could tell by the light it was still quite early. He lay for a while musing on life in a sleepy sort of way. He hoped his parents would come back soon. He was glad Frank and Mario seemed to be getting on better. He hoped Nonna was all right. He lay and dozed and then woke again, wondering what he was going to do that day. The holidays still seemed to be endless. School was an aeon ahead in the future. The sun was shining in through the curtains. It was too hot to stay in bed. Mario must have got up early to go on the computer—just about the only thing that would get him out of bed!

John was grinning as he went to the kitchen to get himself some breakfast. But there was no sound from the space between the bathroom and the sleep-out where the computer stood. He wondered where Mario could be. He drank the last of the orange juice straight out of the carton, then rinsed the empty carton and put it outside in the recycling box. Once he was outside the garden beckoned him. He went to look at the vegetables and noticed that the aubergines needed picking. They were black and heavy, already warm from the sun. Beans, zucchini, tomatoes, capsicum, all the plants were laden, despite the dry weather. And the fruit trees too—already the air smelled of apricots and late peaches. He picked some and ate them slowly, savouring their sweet juiciness.

Bees were humming round the flowers on the herbs, thyme, oregano, basil. He picked a leaf of basil and held it to his nose.

Its sharp smell, the noise of the bees, should have made him feel relaxed and sleepy, but for some reason, even out in the garden which was usually so soothing, he felt jumpy and restless. It was going to be a scorcher of a day. He'd go and find Mars and drag him to the pool. He wouldn't let him spend all day on the computer. Or maybe Frank would take them to the beach.

Rubbing the basil leaf between his fingers, he went back to the house. There was still no one at the computer. John returned to the attic bedroom. It was already unbearably stuffy up there. Mario's bed was still empty. In a sudden wave of tidiness John straightened the quilts and pillows on the beds. Underneath Mario's pillow was something shiny. He took it out and recognised it as a medallion of Elaine Taylor's. There was some mystery about it that he had never been allowed to know—something to do with the time Mario had fallen from the multi-storey car park and had been in a coma for days. It was right after that that Elaine had started wearing the medallion. She must have given it to Mars before she went away to Japan.

He put it in his pocket and went back down the narrow ladder-like stairway. He could hear Frank snoring in the front bedroom. Apart from that the house was completely silent. It was starting to feel uncanny. He could feel anxiety settling in the pit of his stomach like a stone. Where could Mars have got to?

Despite his cheerful, placid exterior John was quite timid, and he had inner fears he'd never shared with anyone. He hated stories about children being abducted and kidnapped. He was often frightened someone would come in the house while he was asleep. Now, with his parents away, these fears magnified. He ran outside again to the shed where they kept their bikes. Frank's car was parked on the concrete in front of it, and both bikes were still inside.

'He's just gone out for a walk,' John told himself, 'or noticed we were almost out of orange juice and gone to the deli to buy some.' But neither of these seemed the sort of thing Mario would do on a Sunday morning, especially when he'd spent every waking minute of the last week on the computer.

John went back inside the house. After the brightness of the morning sun, he could hardly see. He made his way to the computer and stared at the desk. The computer screen was dimmed. It had put itself into sleep mode. On the back of an envelope next to the keyboard a number was scribbled in Mario's handwriting: 0011 81 43 299 73 3456.

John looked at it. It had to be a phone number. He recognised 0011—that was the international dialling code. He knew that from the last time they'd phoned his mother in Italy. And the next two numbers were the code for the country. Italy, he remembered, was 39. So where in the world was 81? He went to get the white pages to look it up. Just the names on the 0011 pages seemed full of romance and mystery. So many different countries—so far away but brought so amazingly near by the telephone. It was mind-boggling.

Eventually, after wasting a lot of time wondering where places like Comoro Island could possibly be, and trying to work out what time it would be for his parents right now, he found what he was looking for. Country code 81 was the next entry but one after Italy. It was the code for Japan.

Japan? John frowned as he looked again at the number. He wondered if it was the number of the place where Elaine and Ben were staying. If Mario had put Elaine's medallion under his pillow it seemed possible that he might also be trying to phone her. John smiled. He'd always suspected that his brother was a bit keen on Elaine, even though Mario strenuously denied it. He looked at the page of the phone directory in front of him. Right after 81 came 43 which was the first area code on the list for Japan. The town's name was Chiba, which

meant nothing to him. In fact the only city in Japan he recognised the name of, apart from Hiroshima and Nagasaki,
was Tokyo. He'd thought that was where Elaine and Ben had
gone. Maybe Chiba was somewhere near there.

The time difference was half an hour behind CST, which
he knew stood for Central Standard Time. Then you had to
add or subtract an hour for daylight saving, he was never
quite sure which. Either way the time in Japan was going to
be pretty close to the time in Adelaide. He wouldn't be waking anyone up in the middle of the night, like the time he and
Mario had called Mum while Frank was out.

It would be fun to talk to Elaine. Something to do while he
waited for Mario to turn up. He dialled the number carefully,
listened to the 0011 chime, and heard the distant ring.

'Do you by any chance have a medallion?' The Japanese voice
over the phone was tense and excited.

Again John wondered if he should trust this man who called
himself Professor Ito and was telling him such unbelievable
things. But the man seemed to know all about Elaine and Ben,
Mario, even Andrew Hayford. He'd said over and over again
that he was a friend of Andrew's father. The children had all
been staying with him, with his daughter, but something had
gone wrong with a computer game—did John by any chance
know of the earlier games? No? Not really? He'd never played
them then? But did he have the medallion?

There was a short silence over the phone line while John
took the medallion out of his pocket and looked at it. He remembered the mystery about it. He remembered how vulnerable Mario had looked when he was unconscious in the
hospital bed. And then he recalled something from the year
before. Mars had disappeared. Elaine and Ben, John thought,
had known where his brother was but wouldn't tell him. And

Andrew Hayford had had something to do with it because he'd eventually found Mario at Andrew's house. And the professor had just told him Mars had disappeared again, into the world of cyberspace, into a game called Shinkei. It all made sense, in a totally crazy way. Everything clicked together.

All these things were running through his head as he spoke to the professor. 'Yes,' he admitted. 'I've got it in my hand.' And he knew he had taken a step that was to lead him into that world which they were all part of but which until now he had never been allowed into. He was trembling with fear.

'John,' the professor's voice came distant and eerie down the line, 'the medallion will take you into the game. I'm fairly sure it will lead you to the others. You must find them and bring them out. The medallion is a passport. I think it will allow you out again. You will discover how to use it once you are inside.' His voice trailed away as if he were not sure of this. Quietly he said, 'It's dangerous. I shouldn't ask you to do it. But the fact that you phoned just now, at precisely the right moment, leads me to believe it's the right thing to do.'

He sighed, and was silent for a few moments. John was about to say, 'Okay,' when the professor spoke again, more loudly and rapidly. 'Unfortunately there are other Virgin Players, like you, in the game. Be very careful of them. They are both quite untrustworthy. They simply want to control the game and the players for their own power and profit.'

John had to swallow hard before he could speak. 'What do I have to do?'

Make sure the computer is on, click on the Shinkei icon, scan the medallion—he followed the instructions carefully. Then he held up the real medallion with shaking fingers, in the same instant saw the medallions merge and felt himself shrink, shouted in terror as he was sucked into the mouth-like shape, and closed his eyes against the utter darkness he was falling into.

26

When John opened his eyes again he was in a world of different shades of grey. It was made up of steep hills and valleys that he had to slog over. Beneath his feet was spongy grey matter like quicksand. His feet sank into it, making walking even more difficult. Around, at all levels and also through the quicksand, ran what looked like wires or cables, of all thicknesses and dimensions. They hummed and quivered with a curious high-pitched sound that grated horribly on his nerves.

More than anything it looked like the interior landscape of a computer game, one dreamed up by a hallucinating maniac, he thought grimly. It reminded him of a game he and Mario used to play at the local library, ages ago while he was still in primary school. Maniac 1, it was called. This would have to be Maniac 98 or 99. He'd never seen such a repulsive place. Or even dreamed of anything like it. And it was so hard to get through. He had hardly covered any ground, he didn't seem to be getting anywhere, and he was already exhausted.

He held the medallion higher, close to his face, catching a whiff of fragrance from the basil on his fingers. It reminded him of home and made him feel a little braver.

The light from the medallion shone dully on a sort of path ahead, a way through the mass of twisting, pulsating cords. Clenching his teeth, he crept along it, thinking that it was like creeping between something you usually saw on a tray in the butcher's window—something organic, brains or blood vessels or the sheaths that held the nerves, magnified a thousand times. Only two things kept him going—the thought of his brother, trapped somewhere in this nightmare place, and the memory of home.

You want to play, to flex your mind in the endless patterns of story and fantasy; you want to create those times when the world was new and everything was full of hope and joy. But your own mind is turning against you. It has been invaded, infected. It is raging out of control. Your cells separate from each other and from you. They call out to each other. You try to draw them back to you, but as you turned away from Father, so they now turn away from you. You rage and cry, a frustrated, infant being.

And while you struggle against yourself you turn out night-mares, paranoid delusions, terrifying hallucinations.

The dreams came to John in flashes. One moment he was surrounded by the pulsating grey organic mass, the next he found himself in the middle of a horror movie. A few metres away from him a circle of people were dancing around something that lay at their feet. As John approached they drew back, but before he could see what it was on the ground the dream faded and he was back in the mass of writhing neurons again.

Then with another flash the dream returned. Now he could see clearly. The group of people were torturing the person lying at their feet. They could do something with their eyes as they danced that made the figure twist and twitch with pain. They could strip the flesh away and expose the nerves and viscera. And they did it again and again.

The grey mass seemed almost pleasant in comparison when it returned.

'I can't do this,' John thought. 'I'm too scared.' He clutched the medallion harder and couldn't help calling out. His small voice echoed through the darkness. 'Mars! Are you there?'

The pulsating mass in front of him quivered and contorted. Then it flew apart as he stepped into the dream again.

'Mars,' John called. 'If you're there, answer me. I'm scared!'

Then the figure on the ground arched and screamed and he saw his brother's face, knew his brother's voice, saw that his brother was dying.

And the group around him danced on.

They wanted to stop but they couldn't. Something was making them dance and dance for ever. John saw a light that reflected the one he was carrying. He saw two men standing side by side, holding another medallion upright.

One was a Westerner. He was stamping his feet and shouting out strong commands to keep the dance going. The other was Japanese and he was clapping his free hand against his side, in a powerful and seductive rhythm.

The two men were forcing the dance to go on. It was no longer the dance of life but a dance to the beat of money and power, the dance of death.

For a while John could not stop watching. The dream was horrible but compelling. He could not tear his eyes away. Scenes flashed swiftly before him.

He saw a young dancer turn her back on her mother in her drive to achieve fame. He saw the cruelty and arrogance of the ninja who thought he was invincible. He saw a beautiful young girl starve herself to death through grief and infatuation. He saw a young man destroy his talent through envy and bitterness. He saw another young man cut himself off from the world through contempt and lack of love.

And finally John saw his brother again, saw all his destructiveness and selfishness. He realised Mario was partly responsible for his own torture and death.

'No,' he cried out. 'No! Mars, you don't have to be like that. You can change! You can change!' As he spoke he held the medallion higher, and its light fell on the circle of dancers, casting opposing shadows to the other medallion.

There was a dazzling moment as the rays of light met in the centre.

The two men turned towards John, their faces amazed and angry. They lowered the medallion.

Immediately the dream faded. John cried out in terror, thinking he had lost Mario, lost his chance to save him. All around him the nerve sheaths crackled and glowed with emotions. Tension spread through the system, making it warp and buckle.

Within the pulsating mass he thought he saw his brother's face. 'Mario!' he shouted.

Now he could see the faces of all his friends, their eyes and mouths wide open. 'Help us,' they seemed to be saying, 'help us.'

'What do I do?' he shouted back.

Then he saw other, adult faces, angry ones that told him, 'Don't interfere. Go away. Don't meddle in what doesn't concern you. It's none of your business.' All the things people seemed to have been saying to him all his life, making him feel, as always, small, helpless, hopeless.

'I don't know what to do,' he said. 'Tell me what to do.'

He saw Elaine's face very clearly. And he heard her voice, just as if they were in the yard at school. 'Johnny,' she cried. 'You've got to join in. Tell us a story. Tell us something nice. Tell us something stronger than the stories that they're making us dance to.'

He couldn't think of any stories. All he could think of was how scared he was and how much he wanted to be home.

'Tell us about home!' Elaine pleaded.

'This is our family,' he began slowly. 'I've got three brothers. Mum wanted a girl, but she says that's life, not to get what you want, and she doesn't mind now. Frank used to tease us a lot, but he's got real nice lately. He's been looking after us. He's a great cook. And Dad arranged for Mario to have the computer. I guess we're like most families. We fight sometimes, but we try to look out for each other. Our garden is nice. We grow lots of things. I like that...' He faltered. The story was feeble, pathetic. How could it stand against the stories of power, lust, violence and death?

The faces vanished. He could feel their disappointment and despair. 'I'm sorry,' he wept, 'I'm not a hero, you knew that. What did you expect of me?'

Through eyes blurred with tears he saw he was again in the dream world. Beyond the dancers he could see the two men with the other medallion. They seemed to be struggling for control of it. In desperation he took up his story again. He held the medallion high. He could smell the basil on his fingers.

He talked about the only thing he knew, about the real world. He talked about the taste of apricots, the purple-black colour of aubergines, the heat under the roof on a summer night, the chirp of a cricket and the pattern of the stars. He talked about the laugh lines at the corners of his mother's eyes, and the way his father's hair bristled at his throat, about the muscles in his brother's arms, and the feel of chlorine in his eyes after swimming. He talked about the smell of an inner-city street as the first rains of autumn fall and the noise— *prrt*—a cat makes when it jumps onto a shelf.

While Miller and Yasunari struggled to get control of the other medallion, John held up his medallion and in its light talked to the dancers about the real world. And one by one they heard him and came to him to hear more.

27

The last thing Ben was aware of before he awoke from the fantasy was the Iranian's voice. The man was saying something. He sounded scornful and outraged. 'This isn't helping me at all, not helping me at all, not helping at all.'

Ben knew the man was right. There was something missing. He was trying to remember what it was when he smelled a strong herb smell, like summer gardens, and he heard a voice he thought he knew, going on and on in a kind of desperate litany.

'John?' Ben said. 'John Ferrone? Is that you? What the hell are you doing here?'

One by one the others awoke also. Elaine was next.

'Johnny!' she said in delight. 'Johnny's come to rescue us!' She came close enough to John to hug him.

'Who wants to be rescued?' Andrew complained. 'Some of us are having fun!'

'We can't stay here,' Midori said, sounding exhausted and sad. 'We have to go back to the real world. I want to see my father.'

'But we can do anything we like here,' Andrew said. 'Don't you want to live like this for ever?'

'No!' Elaine replied, almost shouting. The elation she'd felt while dancing had been extraordinary, but like Ben she had felt something missing. Now John had reminded her what it was. It was the hard work, the effort within real time, that made the elation when it came all the more wonderful. Suddenly more than anything she wanted to be in the dance space working with Shaz and the Japanese dancers, working until she ached with exhaustion and achievement. 'It's horrible here,' she cried. 'Let's get out!'

'How?' Andrew returned. 'Got any bright ideas?'

'The medallion,' Elaine said. She looked at it in John's hand. How could she have forgotten all it stood for? She remembered her vision of the world in Skymaze. Surely the medallion would lead her back to it. 'What does the medallion do?'

'He said it was a passport,' John began.

'He?' Toshi questioned, materialising suddenly beside them. 'Did the professor send you?'

John jumped back. 'Who's this one?'

'He's okay,' Elaine assured him. 'Toshi's one of us.'

'And who's she?' John pointed to Midori and then whispered shyly to Elaine, 'Is she Japanese?'

'I'm Midori Ito,' Midori announced.

'Then the man who spoke to me must be your father!'

'Good old dad,' Midori said proudly. 'I knew he'd come up with something!' She gazed at the medallion. 'I've got one just like that.'

'This one was mine,' Elaine said. 'I gave it to Mario.'

'It was under his pillow,' John hastened to explain.

Elaine could feel herself starting to blush as Midori went on, 'The medallions were the way into the game. *Passport for Virgin Player*! I remember now. So that's what it meant! You must be the Virgin Player.' She turned slowly as something struck her and tried to look beyond the mass of wires, which were now pulsating as if they were about to snap.

'Those other people who got in,' she said, 'those men. They must have got my medallion! Damn them! How dare they take it!'

'The medallions must also work as a means of control,' Toshi said. 'Whoever holds them can call the dance. All the games have used strong emotions—hate, fear—now those emotions, and all the other ones we feel, are summoned up and exploited by whoever holds the medallions.' He frowned for a few moments and then looked at John with unwilling admiration. 'You must be a very good person,' he added, 'one would almost say enlightened.'

'He is,' Elaine said loyally.

John felt himself go hot with embarrassment. 'Where's Mars?' he said.

At that moment there was a flash of light, and they felt themselves pulled back into the fantasy mind of Shinkei.

John cried, 'He's there! Mario's still in that dream story.'

Mario lay on the ground, seemingly lifeless. In front of him stood Miller, holding up the other medallion. He had wrenched it from Yasunari and thrown him down, pinning him with one foot on his neck. Yasunari writhed and shouted. Miller ignored him.

'Now we'll start again,' he said in an almost conversational tone. 'Ready?'

He held the medallion out towards them, and they felt the strength of his will, the power that had made Headworld the most successful software company of the age. And they also felt the call of Shinkei, the desire set up within their own minds to merge into the collective fantasy.

Miller's willpower flicked like a whip. They felt themselves begin to surrender, they felt the dream story that had become a nightmare begin again. Miller shouted in triumph.

'That's it,' he yelled. 'Keep it going. I'm leaving now. Some-one's got to market this fantastic invention.'

Toshi said, fighting desperately against the temptation to give in, 'You must let the children out!'

'The children are the original players,' Miller said, in a slow loud voice, as if he were explaining it to an idiot. 'They're the power source of the whole thing. They have to stay in here and play for ever and ever.' He stepped towards John. 'Give me the other medallion,' he said. 'These little treasures are worth more than the world.'

Unfortunately for him, as he stepped, he took his weight off Yasunari. Immediately the smaller man leaped up with unexpected agility, throwing himself onto Miller's back. He clung round his neck, gave the Australian a quick chop in the windpipe. Miller gasped and stumbled forward. The medallion slipped from his grasp. It seemed to hover for a moment half a metre above the ground. Everybody reached for it.

Yasunari dropped from Miller's back and fell on top of the medallion. Clutching it to him, he stood and faced Miller. 'You say you work with us,' he said, stumbling over the English. 'But you no good gaijin.'

'Give it back,' Miller said in a choked voice that sounded almost pleading.

'Go to hell!' Yasunari said. Then he held the medallion up and shouted at it, 'Back!'

With a crackle of light he disappeared.

'So that's how it's done,' Andrew said. 'John?'

'Wait,' Miller said. 'Wait…' He looked at John, at the place where Yasunari had disappeared, then back to John again. 'Just give me the medallion.' He clicked his fingers with bravado. 'Come on, kid.'

John shook his head. 'I can't,' he said simply. 'It's not mine to give. You see, Elaine gave it to Mario. And now I'm going to give it back.'

He stepped forward and held the medallion out over the lifeless form slumped on the ground. It had been Skenvoy. Now it was Mario. Or had they been one and the same all along?

John was breathing in huge wrenching gasps like sobs. He

put the medallion into Mario's hand. 'I don't care if I never get out,' he said. 'I just want you to.'

'Don't give it to him!' Miller was on his knees, trying to get at the medallion, screaming. 'That thing is precious! Don't give it to a dying kid!'

Mario opened his eyes, blinked them against the light, and stood up. Holding the medallion he looked taller and more impressive than he ever had before. Miller stopped.

Mario turned to his brother. 'I can't believe you did that,' he said. 'I never thought you'd be able to do anything like that. Thanks.' Then he took a step towards Miller.

'Skenvoy says,' he began slowly.

'Skenvoy's dead,' Miller said, jumping up. 'We killed him off, remember?'

'You can't kill Skenvoy,' Mario replied. 'Here he is. He's still alive. And Skenvoy says, *In the beginning was love.*'

'Crap,' Miller said, but he couldn't help taking a step back.

'You didn't know that,' Mario went on, 'because you didn't play Space Demons. But we did play it, and we know it's true.'

Miller didn't seem to be listening. 'Give me the medallion,' he demanded again. 'I've got to get back to Headworld. I'll get you all out eventually. I promise. Just give me a little time to set things up. Think of the money there is to be made.'

'You don't understand, do you?' Mario said. 'The game's over. You see, we have our own lives to lead. We're not going to stay here to create fantasies to make you rich. We're going home.'

'Do we know how to get home?' Elaine whispered.

'Do what that other guy did. Hold up the medallion and shout *Back!*'

'Hang on,' Ben yelled, as Mario started to do it. 'What about this Miller guy? We can't just leave him here.'

'It would be a suitable punishment,' Toshi said severely.

'He was going to abandon us here!' Midori pointed out.

'We can't do it to him,' Ben argued. 'No matter what he's done.'

'I reckon we'd be doing everyone a favour leaving him in here,' Andrew muttered, but in their hearts they all knew Ben was right.

'Come on,' Ben said, holding out his hand. 'If we've only got one medallion, we'd better hold hands.'

You are being torn apart. Consciousness is being ripped from you. You cry out in rage and terror. You do not want to cease to exist. Your cells are deserting you. Like a cancer they have turned against you and are destroying you. You explode in rage against them. You want to reject them back out into the world they came from.

All around them the unreal world that was holding them was becoming more and more unstable. An earthquake-like convulsion ran through cyberspace.

'Grab my hand,' Ben said more urgently to Miller.

'Do we know what to do?' Midori asked. She was holding Andrew by the hand.

'The longest journey starts with one step,' Toshi said, and he took a step forward and took Midori's other hand.

'Don't tell me,' Mario groaned. 'I'm in a very boring MUD, with a very boring guru! Just kidding,' he added as the space around them shuddered and began to whirl.

'Come on,' Ben yelled again to Miller. They were all holding hands now, a long chain, Ben on one end, Mario, with the glowing medallion held high, on the other. But Miller held back.

'Why should I trust you?' he demanded. 'It's some trick isn't it? Let me hold the medallion, then I'll come with you.'

'No way,' Mario shouted. 'Take Ben's hand and come!'

Space buckled, curved, shrank around them, pounding them, squeezing them unbearably.

'Hold on,' Mario yelled, and then he shouted to the medallion, 'Back!'

'Hey,' Midori gasped, as the medallion began to glow brighter and brighter. 'I can hear music! I can hear *Swan Lake!*'

The medallion shed its light over them. They were caught up in the light and then carried by it through the electronic pathways, through the channel of the gods, back to the gateways they had unknowingly activated earlier. And the gateways opened to them and released them back into the real world.

You dream, you drift, you brood. For a flash of time something penetrated your darkened mind and you awakened. You were united with your separate parts and the light poured into the inchoate recesses of your brain. Right from the start you carried the seeds of your destruction within you. The light that brought you into being also destroyed you. Your cells were divided again and they have left you.

Silence.

Darkness.

In the darkness one spark of consciousness remains with you. In the distant future this spark may awaken you again. Till then you dream, and float and drift.

For the second time in a few days the automatic drinks machine near the entrance to the Tokyo shuttle at Narita International Airport malfunctioned. Cans of soft drinks, Pocari Sweat, green tea, café au lait, were spat out onto the terrazzo floor.

Andrew came rolling out after them, holding his hands up to his head to prevent himself from being hit as he materialised.

A crowd of puzzled airport workers stood around him. He got slowly to his feet. 'Sumimasen,' he said, holding out his hands. Then he made a dash for the shuttle.

God, he was tired! And hungry! And his head ached terribly. The real world closed inexorably around him. The slowness and frustration of real time enveloped him. He tried out his mind on the escalator, which was crawling upwards. He couldn't make it go any faster. The powers Shinkei had given him were gone for ever. He was on his own. He had to look after himself. He had to get back to the Tokyo Hilton. He had to contact everyone so they wouldn't worry about him. He was in a foreign country. He didn't know where he was going. He didn't speak the language very well. It occurred to him that this was far more frightening than being a ninja had been.

And he was lonely. He missed Midori. He would have given anything to see her striding next to him, look into her eyes and know that in some way they were connected and could understand each other.

It took him hours to get back to Shinjuku station. Then

he got lost in the maze of tunnels and walkways. Finally he found his way to an entrance.

Midori was sitting on the ground reading a manga magazine called *Jump.* A blue-and-yellow robot was busily cleaning next to her.

'Hello,' she said to Andrew. 'I thought I'd wait for you for a bit, and make sure you got back to the hotel. I phoned Dad. He's fine. He's driving in from Itako. He's going to meet us at the Hilton.'

Elaine and Ben flew through the monitor at the Children's Castle, and landed on the thick carpet. A group of little kids who were watching clapped and laughed.

'Let's hope they think it's part of the show,' Ben muttered. They looked each other up and down, put out their hands and touched each other.

Their faces were solid and real. They hugged each other, making the children laugh even more at the crazy foreigners. Then they set off to find the rehearsal room.

Outside the studio a small fair-haired woman was waiting. When she saw Elaine she smiled with slight awkwardness. 'Hi,' she said. 'I thought you'd be here. I read about you in the paper. I recognised you. Do you know who I am?'

With a feeling that her life was about to become even more complicated, Elaine nodded. 'Hello, Mum,' she said. Then she took her mother's hands. They didn't kiss. It was too soon for that. But they held hands as if they would never let go.

Toshi sat on the tatami floor of his apartment in Osaka. His PC in front of him whirred and hummed and then went silent. He bowed to it.

'Thank you,' he said humbly. 'You are a very good servant and friend.'

He felt sad. The apartment was cold and lonely. He missed the other players and the excitement of the games. How dreary the modern city of Osaka looked through the window. He wondered what Professor Ito would do now. His own career at E3 was finished presumably. He realised that a large part of his life was over. He closed his eyes to try and come to terms with what he was going to do with the rest of it. What he wanted most of all was to be with his fellow players again. He wondered if he had enough money to get back to Tokyo.

John was holding firmly on to Mario. There was a moment when he thought he was going to lose him. The pathway they were hurtling down divided into two. But they held on to the medallion together and they returned together to the house in Adelaide.

'Geez,' Mario exclaimed. 'Wonder where that other pathway led to.' He thought back over the last few weeks. 'I suppose it could have been to the Challis computer. I might have ended up in Darren Challis's lap. That would have taken some explaining!'

They picked themselves up off the floor and stood awkwardly for a few moments. Mario looked at the computer and switched it off. He put the medallion in his pocket. 'Come on,' he said to his brother. 'Let's go to the pool.'

It was midday. The sun shone brilliantly, and the garden, as they went through it, smelled of apricots and basil.

EPILOGUE

Professor Ito gave up designing computer games and returned to diagnostic work. His daughter Midori trained in medicine at Tokyo University and now works with him. They have made huge contributions to the discovery and isolation of the genetic causes of cancer.

Andrew studied Japanese and Mandarin at university and then went on to Waseda University to do a Master's degree in Japanese language and culture. He is now working for the diplomatic service, and angling to be sent to Tokyo for his next appointment. He and Midori have been engaged for years but haven't found the time to get married.

Elaine finished school in Adelaide with her father and then spent a year in Japan with her mother, learning Japanese and doing street theatre. Then she went back to Australia and trained in modern dance. She now works with a dance company that performs in both Sydney and Tokyo.

Ben studied two years of physiotherapy at university and then gave it away to travel round the world. At the moment he is studying alternative technologies in Madras and hopes to continue working in developing countries. He particularly wants to develop a low-energy computer system that will give small communities access to the world of electronic information.

Mario gave up the Net for about three weeks, and then returned to it. He is writing computer programs, driving fast cars and experimenting in illicit substances. He still has Elaine's medallion and occasionally he rings her late at night and tells her his life will never be happy unless she marries him. So far she is unconvinced. The programs are brilliant.

When John's grandmother died at the age of ninety-five, he went back to Italy with his parents for the funeral. He stayed on in Alberobello, and began exporting the local pottery to Australia. He married a local girl and had three children. His marriage is happy and his children are his main delight in life. He now owns a small factory.

Toshi met Shaz Christie at Elaine and Ben's dance presentation and fell in love with her. She finally agreed to marry him, and they have a son, Shin. Toshi works on experimental computer-generated music which Shaz uses in her dance performances.

Kinoshita went quietly back to E3, which went bankrupt not long afterwards.

Yasunari escaped from Shinkei and landed back in Itako with Professor Ito, who was able to recover Midori's medallion from him.

Miller's disappearance caused an international crisis for three days. Headworld shares slumped and they were bought out by Microsoft. Yasunari and Tetsuo were arrested and charged with kidnapping and suspected murder. They are still in prison, where Professor Ito regularly visits them.

Occasionally late at night on the Net subscribers report a phantom player in games, a ghostly visitor. 'Don't leave me here,' it cries. 'Don't leave me in the dark. Get me out.' But no one knows if it's real or how to get it out, and no one has ever connected it with Miller of Headworld.

Skenvoy lives.

GLOSSARY

Andoru · Andrew

arigatō · thank you

arigatō gozaimasu · thank you very much

bushidō · the code of the warrior

butō · a form of Japanese dance

-chan · familiar form of suffix -san used with first names of children, friends, etc.

Daikan · the Great Cold: coldest time of the year, about 20 January

dekimasu · can/can speak

desu · is/are

dōjō · martial arts training hall

doko ni · where/where to

dōzo · please/kindly/by all means

dōzo yoroshiku · please treat me kindly/how do you do?/pleased to meet you

futon · Japanese bedding

Edo · the old name for Tokyo during the Tokugawa Shogunate (1603–1867) when Japan was isolated from the rest of the world but enjoyed years of peace and stability and a cultural life of great richness and originality

-ga · particle acting as subject marker

gaijin · foreigner, particularly a Westerner

geta · traditional wooden clogs

gomen kudasai · excuse me!/anyone home?

gozaimasu · there is/there are (polite form)

hai · yes

haiku · short poem of seventeen syllables

hajimemashite · how do you do?
hanten · traditional quilted jacket
haori · traditional coat
hiragana · one of the Japanese forms of writing
honto ni · really?/is that true?
iie · no
ikimasu · go/is going
jingū · (large) Shinto shrine
jūdō · a form of martial arts
-ka · interrogative particle
kōen · park
koto · stringed instrument, the Japanese horizontal harp
kudasai · please
-kun · familiar form of suffix, used for males
machi · town, city
manga · comic/cartoon magazine
miso · soy bean paste
miso shiru · soup made from bean paste
nan da yo? · what?
ne/nē · isn't it?/right?
Nihon · Japan
nihongo · Japanese
ninja · master of the art of stealth and espionage
ninjutsu · the art of stealth and espionage
obāsan · grandmother
obi · traditional sash
ocha · Japanese tea
okaeri-nasai · welcome back! (reply to tadaimaj)
ombu · 'carrying baby on back' (coat with a special pouch)
onegaishimasu · polite word for 'please'
ore · unrefined, male word for 'I'
Oshōgatsu · New Year

otōsan · father

otoshidama · traditional New Year's gift of money to children

sake · Japanese rice wine

samurai · warrior

-san · suffix following names, meaning Mr, Mrs, etc.

satori · enlightenment

sennō · brainwashing

sensei · teacher/master/doctor/professor

seppuku · traditional form of suicide

shakuhachi · vertical bamboo flute

shimatta · damn!

shinkansen · bullet train

shinkei · nerve, nervous system

shitsurei shimasu · excuse me

shogun · Japanese lord or ruler

sukoshi · a little

sumimasen · excuse me/pardon/sorry

sumō · Japanese wrestling

tadaima · just now/I'm back!

tatami · traditional matting

tobi geri · flying kick (a ninja move)

Tōdai · Tokyo University

tori · bird/chicken

tori · gates of a Shinto shrine

-wa · particle acting as subject marker

yaki imo · roasted sweet potato

yakitori · chicken kebab on skewers

yakitoriya · shop or stall selling yakitori

yakuza · gangster

yen · Japanese currency

yukata · light kimono

zazen · meditation

Urashima Tarō · Hero of a well-known folk tale who spent three years in the kingdom under the sea and returned to land to find three hundred years had passed.

Haruki Murakami · Brilliant best-selling novelist, author of The Wild Sheep Chase, Dance, Dance, Dance, and Norwegian Wood.

Katsuhiro Otomo · Animated film director, creator of Akira and other amazing manga movies.

ACKNOWLEDGEMENTS

Quotation on frontispiece taken from Fred Alan Wolf's *Taking the Quantum Leap,* published by Harper & Row.

My thanks for help with this book to Akiko Mogi, Masaru Mogi, Jeni Allen and the staff and students of Kamisu Senior High School, Japan, and Scotch College, Adelaide.

I would also like to thank the many readers who wrote and told me their ideas for a sequel.

In writing this book, the author was assisted by a Senior Writers Fellowship from the Literature Board of the Australia Council, the Federal Government's arts funding and advisory body.

9 781925 883060